H. R. F. Keating, a Fellow of ... e,
w... s.
H... n
... nt
as
or
de
...er

D1342313

5/5/22

BUS

Please renew or return items by the date
shown on your receipt

www.hertfordshire.gov.uk/libraries

Renewals and enquiries: 0300 123 4049
Textphone for hearing or 0300 123 4041
speech impaired users:

L32 11.16

Hertfordshire

52 426 685 5

sh

am

be

ive

'An engaging and ... *Guide*

A
KIND
OF
LIGHT

H. R. F. KEATING

ENDEAVOURINK

AN ENDEAVOUR INK PAPERBACK

This paperback edition published in 2017
by Endeavour Ink
Endeavour Ink is an imprint of Endeavour Press Ltd
Endeavour Press, 85-87 Borough High Street,
London, SE1 1NH

Copyright © H. R. F. Keating 1987

The right of H. R. F. Keating to be identified as the author of
. this work has been asserted by her in accordance with the
Copyright, Design and Patents Act, 1988

All rights reserved. No part of this publication may be
reproduced, stored in a retrieval system, or transmitted, in
photocopying, recording or otherwise, without the prior
permission of the copyright owner

ISBN 978-1-911445-43-2

Printed and bound in Great Britain by
Clays Ltd, St Ives plc

www.endeavourpress.com

CHAPTER 1

This morning I smelt Africa.

Thomasina le Mesurier looked at the words she had written in her neat copperplate hand. There they were, purple-grey in indelible pencil, on the first page of the first of the dozen Pocket Memoranda books she had bought at the lithographer's near the Royal Geographical Society's rooms on one of her visits to London from Salisbury. Already almost forgotten Salisbury.

Above her, sullen black clouds had gathered threatening imminent rain. Beneath her feet the engines of the vessel creeping her way down the coast throbbed wearisomely, as they had throbbed with dull monotony for the past seven weeks. But nothing could dampen the uprush of spirits she felt. Coming on deck at first light to rid herself of the suffocating air of her cabin, she had found in her nostrils, sudden and rich, that new aroma, brought to her by the heavy warm breeze, herald of the storm to come.

She sniffed it in once more, an amalgam of dark rich Forest odours emanating from the almost black, dense green rim of the nearby coast. Then she returned to the memoranda book (of just the sort Mr Galton's *Art of Travel* recommended) resting on the broad rail of the wallowing steamship.

This morning I smelt Africa. Dear Doctor Diver, my dear, dead friend, now is the very moment to open the journal I have promised myself to keep. The journal I would have shown to you, with trembling modesty. On my return from this Africa that I have watched these many days slipping by, mysterious, forbidding, but, oh, how magnetic. This journal that may at last record my success in the search I am undertaking in your stead, my dear, good, dead friend and mentor, or my failure. The recovery of that wondrous plant, snatching it out of savagedom and bringing it back to the civilised world where it will cure the terrible scourge from which you yourself in the end perished. The plant which you collected all those years ago, little knowing at that moment its virtue. I see it now as you described it to me so many times during our rambles through our Wiltshire meadows. Its clover-shaped leaves, yet clover magnified one hundred times in the steamy magic of the Great Forest, and the deep, glossy green of them. I see, too that patch of watery swamp where they grew, fed by that unmistakable – so you often said – little waterfall divided into three by a fang-like yellow rock. There, and there alone, you believed they flourished, the plants that you found had accidentally saved you in your first bout of that terrible illness, only to be destroyed by yourself in your delirium. Shall I ever reach that place? Can I, a woman and alone, – but you, too, were alone – reach a place it cost you so dear to arrive at?

By the grace of him above I shall achieve that end, I promise. I promise you, dear Doctor Diver, who so obstinately would always deny the existence of a Divinity, that if earnest endeavour can take me to that place, through whatever dangers there may be, it shall do so. I shall. I shall pluck out at last those plants, conserve them till I come back to a world where it can be proved that they will end for ever the dread scourge that deprived me within one black month of you, my old, dear, secret friend, and of a mother as dear. I name it. The typhoid fever.

Oh, heavens, rain. A shower is beating towards us across the grey, heaving sea. But what a shower! A rain-pour to knock all English drenchers into so many cocked hats. I will write more. But shelter now!

***

David Teigh lifted up his head and sang.
"Sex beneath the shower
 That's the magic hour
Till soap gets in your eyes.
Life's one big surprise.
Soap gets in your eyes."
The water beat down on his loose black curls, streamed across his broad handsome Irish face.
'Tom,' he called out after a little. "Tom…"
From the bedroom there was no answer.

He poked his head out beyond the shower curtain.

"Teresa Olivia Mountjoy," he proclaimed in his voice-of-God voice, "I summon you to the soap-slippery presence."

"No. Listen Teigh, I've got an idea."

David groaned, dying-actor style.

"No," Tom called back from the bed where she sat, duvet hunched round her, a welter of Sunday papers spreading beyond. "Listen I may be on to something."

Redoubled groan.

"No, hold on, Teigh, you have ideas every five minutes."

"Yes, but my ideas don't get put into practice. Whereas…"

"Get out of that damn shower and come in here where I can talk to you. This may change our whole lives."

"And you turn down soapy sex for that?"

"Well, not our whole lives. But next year maybe. More for you actually."

David came padding in, a towel across his shoulders. Dollops of water fell on to the pale carpet. Tom had a section of the *Sunday Messenger* propped on her knees.

"It's this *Jungle Diary of a Victorian Gentlewoman* thing they've been running," she said. "Listen."

Compact, serious in every inch of her dark-eyed tanned, solidly wedge-shaped face beneath the cap of springy hair – the face that delighted television viewers by the million – she skimmed a finger down the paper's close columns.

"No, philosophising… ah, here."

I must have been lying for above a quarter of an hour in my pool of clear rainwater held between that mighty tree's buttresses, letting the damp mud slip from my limbs, soothing my neck after the attentions of that collar of leeches, hardly thinking any thoughts, when I became aware that I was not, as I had believed alone. Alone, of course, save for the ever-present million insects and in the leafy heavens above the monkeys and the birds, busy at their tasks of food gathering, of combining with the flowers in the high tree world to procreate and spread their seed, of mating in that endless round of life-renewal and death-concluding that is

7

the Forest's existence. I was being watched from where my buttress screens did not protect me by other eyes than these. I had been so, I knew at once, for almost as long as I had bathed in the tub which nature had so conveniently filled for me.

I rolled in the clear, lapping water. And I saw him. I have come to call him Atembogunjo, the name he tells me he had before he left his village. He was as naked as I was myself, and his virile member was as erect as those of the apes I have seen mating in the Forest – that sight which when I first came upon it those many months ago disturbed me so greatly. But all such false modesty I have long ago lost.

More, I responded to Atembogunjo. I, who had thought that having reached my thirtieth year I was never able to experience that fever, more terrible than any of the fevers I have endured in the Forest, that fever called love, responded in a lightning-flash, come-from-nowhere immediacy.

So it was that my new life began. My life with Atembogunjo.

How strange that, turning the page to set down a new sentence, I find I have come to the very end of this memoranda book, the sixth I have filled since writing those words, as I remember them, 'This morning I smelt Africa'. Yet it is strangely fitting that now I should have to commence a new volume. I am commencing a new life, a different, altogether unexpected life, which will yet, I am certain, be mine for as long as I shall live now. It will be fully the life that the Forest has slowly and insidiously taught me to live. It is, surely, the meaning, hidden and obscure, of all that has happened to me since I first stepped among the towering trees. My life with Atembogunjo.

Tom looked up at David, eyebrow raised interrogatively.

"Victorian gentlewoman, hey," David said.

"Oh, well come on. That's just the title some smart publisher gave it, their idea of a subtle sexy hint. But it's not the sex that's the really interesting thing."

"You could have fooled-"

"No, Teigh. Don't you see? *"Now I should have to commence a new volume"*. She must have gone on putting it all down. The jungle life. All of it. The living as well as the sex. As seen by a pair of pre-Freudian but jolly sharp eyes."

"So? Next week: Part Two"

8

"Oh, no. didn't you read the puffs? Part Two's still hidden in the rainforest. A man prospecting for something or other, there in the hot green depths, apparently found all Thomasina le Mesurier's memoranda books, stashed away in some sort of cairn or something. But – and this is the point – he could only carry off half a dozen of them. Or he only wanted to. So the rest are still there."

"Oh God," David said. "You're going off to find them."

"Of course. It's a bloody good story, and it'll make a bloody good documentary. Much better than that awful *New Woman of the Kasbah* that B-J's so keen for me to do."

"And changing my life? You were kindly going to do that, remember?"

"Oh, but yes. You're coming with me. You're going to jack in the B.B.C., like you say about twice a week you want to, and B-J's going to take you on as director."

"Oh, thank you. Thank you very much."

David stood looking down at Tom and the sprawl of papers on the bed.

"Well," he said, "have to think about it, won't I? Um. And incidentally, would you marry me?"

"Certainly not. Christ, whatever put that into your head?"

"Don't know just suddenly thought. You, changing my whole life perhaps. And we have been together for three years now. I might be the right person for you to settle down with. Hmm?"

"No hmm. Not even the faintest trace of hmm."

"No? Well, thought I'd ask. Before we plunge off into the primeval jungle."

"So we are plunging?"

"Oh, well, of course. I mean, if one's going to change the whole course of one's life, one ought to do it on the spur of the moment."

CHAPTER 2

Thomasina sat facing the priest across the rough wooden table on the veranda of his mission house. His face glistened with the unhealthy sweat of fever. His washed blue eyes shone in pale intensity. His large pointed, white-tipped nose seemed almost to quiver with hot emotion.

"My child," he said in the whispery French Thomasina was finding it such an effort to follow, "is there nothing I can say that will deter you?"

"Father- Monsieur, I – I understand, or believe that I do, your concern. But I am here under a promise. I have pledged myself to go through the rainforest until I find that plant which will bring such benefit to mankind. Can you not see that it is my duty to go?"

"Duty? Oh, my poor child. A duty to find some plant of possible medicinal value? My child there can be only one good reason for venturing into the Forest. That is to save the heathen in their ignorance. To bring order to lives lost in wildness and debauchery. And you think to risk your immortal soul by going there to secure some pieces of root. Your immortal soul."

Thomasina could not repress a quick frown, reflecting the distaste such language produced in her.

"Monsieur, Father," she said, "surely you - what shall I say? Surely you exaggerate. Or at least you are being cautious to excess on my behalf. I have told you: my old friend, Doctor Diver, went through the Forest for month after month some twenty years ago to add to the sum of human knowledge, and he survived with his immortal soul - well, that is to say, he was not a believer. But he emerged from the Forest, if not as well in body, as sane and good as he went into it."

"Not a believer?"

The priest pounced, fleshy white-tipped nose descending. "My child, only now do you admit this. You have been in the hands of an atheist. You have been caught in the toils of Satan. My child, I forbid you to go one step further."

Thomasina felt rebellion rise up in her, a gush of pure red blood.

"Father, I do not wish to be disrespectful. But I cannot yield to such a prohibition. Not from you, not from - from anyone of your religious persuasion. I - I am the daughter of a canon of the Church of England, and I think I have learned what my duty is and where it should take me."

"And you conceive that this duty leads you into the Forest? My poor child, you can have no idea of the danger there is for you there. Oh, I do not mean the leopards, the snakes, the venomous insects. I do not even mean the cannibal tribes, the natives with their poison-tipped arrows. No, these may do no more than take your life. The danger I speak of is far more terrible. It is a danger to the spirit. It is your soul that you would put in peril. Of course, this Doctor – Doctor - whatever he was called, of course he escaped. He had lost his soul already. But you, my child, you are an innocent. You cannot go there."

Thomasina clenched her mouth into a hard pout.

"Yet I intend to."

Wearily the priest shook his head. "Oh you still do not understand. How should you, brought up in that terrible religion of yours. I know it. Do not think I do not. I have met too many of your Englishmen who boasted of their famous Protestantism. Of their liberty, as they like to call it."

He leant forward across the thick unplaned wood of the table, his hands stretched pale and taut on its surface.

"My daughter, you must learn. Mother Church was given to mankind so that we might have rules to guide us, to keep us from such dangers as you are wantonly going towards. Rules by which we can preserve our souls in safety."

"But - but, monsieur, I do not accept those rules. I was, yes brought up a Protestant. And, as such I was taught that obedience should be voluntary. Only what is freely conceded is true obedience."

"No. That is heresy."

"No. No. I reject your church, with all its dictates, its rituals that aim to bind every person to its least whim. I reject its threats and its torments. I stand on liberty, as I have been taught to do from my earliest days."

"Liberty? Liberty? I tell you there never was liberty in the act of our creator in bringing this world into existence. It was a world created in obedience to law. Liberty, the liberty you dare to cherish, is revolt. Revolt against Almighty God. It is the wilful seeking of disorder, no less. It is sin, the worst of sins."

"No."

Thomasina heard her voice rise almost to a shriek in the velvety African air. With a pull of effort she regained command of herself.

"Father," she said, "I do not think we have any more to say to each other. I concede you are sincere in your beliefs concerning the Forest. But I cannot acknowledge that there will be any such danger as you speak of if I go there with good intentions. And I do go with such intentions. I mean to find that plant my friend – my good friend and mentor – Doctor Diver knew to be a cure for the most terrible of plagues. I intend to find it, and to bring it back for the good of all mankind."

She pushed herself up from the table. Only now did she see that it had been speckled with the transparent wings discarded by flying ants. She felt as if she was rising up from chains.

The priest turned his washed blue eyes to her.

"My daughter," he said, "one day in your madness you will remember my words. Remember them as a soul in hell remembers."

***

"No, it can't be worth it," David Teigh said. "It bloody can not."

In the moist heat of the N'Djili airport, under the bluey-grey light of the handful of neon tubes dangling from the roof, some not working, he groaned aloud.

But Tom Mountjoy's solid wedge of a face under her tight cap of hair was alight with uncomplicated joy.

"Nonsense," she said. "It's lovely. Total confusion. Inextricable chaos. It's what travel ought to be."

Repeated groan.

"And I can tell you who would have revelled in it," Tom went on.

"Your precious Miss le Mesurier? I don't know so much about that."

"Oh, yes, she would. There's a lot of fizz there, under all the Victorian decorum. Look at the way she dealt with that oozy French priest in the end."

"Yeah I suppose so."

David looked round at the Arrivals area once more. At the long bunched line of waiting passengers, some hopefully still clutching bags, others moodily kicking theirs along in front of them. At the rubbish-strewn, oil-puddled concrete floor. At the dark African night beyond the huge open doors behind them.

"All the same," he said, "I'm beginning to wish you'd never read those damn diaries. Or, no, I really wish that your bloody mystery-figure prospector had never found the cairn or whatever it is where they're hidden. Or, anyhow, that he'd had the decency to leave the things where they were. Wherever that's going to turn out to be."

"Oh, come on Teigh, don't be such a drag. A lot must have gone wrong when you were making films before."

"No, nothing did. Nothing ever went wrong. Or if it did Auntie B.B.C. just waved her magic wand, which I may say simply dripped with licence-payers' money, and all was put right."

Ahead, beyond the bulgy line of passengers stuck at passport control, they could see a second line, equally held up at customs.

"Jesus," David said, "do you see what that chap's doing at the table through there? He's counting some poor devil's handkerchiefs. Actually counting the whole pile of them, with the fellow's luggage spread all over the place. Are they going to do that to us?"

"Wouldn't be surprised," Tom said. "They'll probably count all your malaria pills, too, one by one. Snitch a few as well."

A voice, English, female, precise and patently expressing shock, addressing some innocent fellow passenger, floated back to them.

13

"Did nobody tell you anything in London? Don't you know you have to bring cigarettes to get through customs?"

"And I didn't bring a single packet," David said, depression edging his voice. "So how long will they keep us here, for God's sake?"

"Oh, till morning, I dare say. Or till those chaps finish their shift. What's it matter? We're in Africa. Africa. Didn't you smell it on the way over from the plane? Just what I smelt when I did my Kilimanjaro film. Heat, the earth, the plants, bit of African skin, too. Sweet, hot, ripe."

"Very romantic. But look at it. Look at us. Look at Reg Blandy through there. Call him a cameraman?"

Reg Blandy, small, scanty-haired, neat in khaki bush-shirt and khaki shorts, sharply creased, had got through the passport check ahead of them. Already he had taken over a corner of the barn-like hall beyond. He had laid out a grey blanket, and on it he was arranging his cameras, their stock of film, his numerous accessories, making a little tick every now and again in a spiral notebook.

"Jesus," David said, "what sort of footage are we going to get from someone like that?"

"Oh, it won't be too bad. Reg was a go-getter in his day. So they say."

David produced another groan, yet more theatrical.

"And mutton-head," he said. "Josh. What about him? Sound man? I bet he's only called that because he's a sound man when it comes to doing the nice safe thing."

"Very funny. And for Christ's sake shut up. He's only just behind us."

Josh Perkins, tall, broad-shouldered, but undeniably moon-faced under his thatch of blond hair, had let come between them a huge African, in a sail-like scarlet shirt decorated with white lightning streaks, and his equally large wife, a flamboyant purple and green garment wrapped tight across magnificent bosom and pasture-lush hips. Their children, two or three, perhaps four, were darting about, leaving and returning to the mother craft like so many bustling pilot-boats.

"I mean," David went on, "is he touched or something, Josh? Have you worked with him before? God, I tried to chat at Heathrow and couldn't get a word out of him."

"Yup, I've worked with him. Once. He's okay, actually. But you know what sound-men are like. Worlds of their own. I knew one once who was quietly convinced he was going to be called to Brazil one day, I think it was Brazil, to be made emperor. Perfectly all right, till you were stupid enough to mention Latin America."

"Which no doubt you frequently did."

"Well, it was interesting, in a way."

"So, this is going to be interesting, too, I suppose. A cameraman for ever laying out bits and pieces of his stuff and ticking them off in a little notebook and a sound man who thinks he's the emperor of Peru."

"Brazil, actually. And that was another sound man, not Josh"

"Probably much of a muchness and he and Reg are all we've got, all your wonderful B-J would pay for. They'd have a screaming fit at the B.B.C. if anyone wanted them to make a film like this."

"Oh, come on. When you were there you did nothing but moan about all the rules and regulations. Hampering the great artistic freedom. The fine, wild spirit. So where's the fine wild spirit now?"

"I don't know. Still sitting in the plane most likely. If not back in London, wailing outside the windows at the television centre like Heathcliff begging to be let back in."

He shuffled forward another two feet in the sprawling queue.

"*In the Steps of a Jungle Gentlewoman*," he said. "I never dreamt it was going to be like this. Do you know, we stand about as much chance of getting to those hidden diaries as ending up an old married couple falling asleep over the cocoa."

***

Thomasina, lying under the shroud of the mosquito net on the crudely-made bed in the mission guest hut – she wished she could have done other than accept that much hospitality from Père Jossuet

– slept worse than she had done on any night since she had set foot in Africa. The pale priest's words of warning came back to her again and again.

Was she wrong, despite her furious rejection of all he had said, to have come here? Had she, a year ago, seen altogether too much in the legacy that Doctor Diver had bequeathed her? That unexpectedly large sum? And, more, those volumes of his Notes?

Had it perhaps never even entered his head that she would see his gift as a request from the grave to undertake the task he had been unable in his long years of uncertain health to perform himself? Had he never so much as dreamt that she, a woman and weak, would attempt to follow the Forest paths he had travelled with such hardship to vindicate his belief in the plant he had once possessed.

And did the Forest truly hold mysterious terrors, unmentionable wildnesses, that once she had set foot in it, would enmesh her?

But in all the many talks she had had with the Doctor he had never once spoken of the danger Père Jossuet had so insisted on. There had not been one word in all the years since the day when, aged twelve, wandering at a little distance from her parents on a country ramble, examining with curiosity a wild flower she had not seen before, he, gently botanising in his turn, had explained to her, without the formality of an introduction, why the flower grew where it did, how it had come to be as it was.

Dangers of other sorts, in talking of his expedition into the Dark Continent, he had told her of often enough. Hippopotamuses that could easily take it into their heads to upset your canoe – your pirogue, as they were called, - as you were paddled further and further into the interior. The somehow sickening sound of a leopard coughing in the night in the Forest depths. Leeches that sensed the passing of a warm body and attached themselves to exposed flesh in a desperate need for blood. The huge trees that, shallow-rooted, could sometimes almost without warning crash devastatingly to the ground. The spike-lined pits, cunningly concealed, in which natives caught animals for meat and into which it was all too easy to fall.

But about any spiritual danger, in all the years of their adult secret friendship, the old Doctor had been perfectly silent. True, he had told her of the strain of the loneliness as, solitary, he had journeyed to fill his glass-sided Wardian specimen cases and his collecting boxes with ever more new and unrecorded species. He had spoken of going for day upon day with no more than the simple exchanges which it was possible to hold with native paddlers or guides. He had prepared her for that hazard.

Or, she thought suddenly, had his talk of the necessity of the traveller taking with him some solid literary nourishment been, not advice, but mere reminiscence?

Had he been unable to speak of those deeper ills that so perturbed Père Jossuet? Had he once perhaps been near to succumbing to an inner horror? And had he not had the courage to revive even the thought of that during any of their many hours of talk over the years?

And if he had felt that horror, if Père Jossuet was right or even partly right, then should she indeed be here? Had she, in truth, then wasted all she had done since she had learnt from Doctor Diver's attorney of his will? Since she had decided then and there in that office in Castle Street to abandon the quiet, ordered Salisbury life, those modest family ways kept up unvaryingly after the peaceful passing of her father? To abandon in a moment that order and quietude and to undertake to go alone to Africa, to the very heart of its jungle, to find again that healing plant the Doctor had discovered. The same plant he had been unable to bring home. She still remembered his anguish as he told her of that moment when, emerging from delirium, he knew he had survived the deadly fever but that he no longer possessed the plant that had cured him – that horrible moment when he realised that it could only have been he, himself who, at the height of his fever had destroyed it.

Was she indeed labouring under a delusion? Had the ending within a single month under the scourge of that same typhoid fever of the two ties she valued most, her mother and her secret friend, utterly impaired her judgment?

She saw then, lying tossing to and fro in the thick hot darkness, her mother in her death-bed agony in the quiet house in the Close, her home for so many years. And she heard again – try to cast it from her mind as she would – the oaths that had come spewing from those frail lips. From lips she had never before heard utter other than comfortable words of everyday talk and – how often – quietly pious words of prayer.

Where had those swaggering, vile pirate words come from to have found lodging in that mild head? But there they had been. To burst out at last, screechingly, in the hushed sickroom, till she herself had been constrained to run to the door to make sure neither of the servants was within earshot.

And now they were there, those selfsame, foul unforgettable expressions, this time in her own head. Would they be launched one day in the depths of the Forest as she wandered victim of that madness Père Jossuet had put so forcefully before her? Could that happen? Would that happen? Should she expose her mind to that appalling risk?

If she could sleep, perhaps she would be able to weigh the issues next day in a sane, calm light. See her expedition as the reasonable undertaking she had hitherto believed it to be, or realise that she was indeed recklessly courting dangers far worse than she had at all known of. But sleep she could not.

Oh, my dear friend, I have been in such a pickle – and have had it so happily resolved. Two days ago, just after I had made my last entry in these pages, Père Jossuet, who conducts the Roman mission here, was kind enough solemnly to take me aside and to warn me in the most hell-fiery terms against even so much as setting foot within the Forest. He meant nothing but my good. But the chief result of his earnest exhortations was to unsettle me to an altogether fearful extent. I spent a wretched night. I was no better by day, and not much better, though exhausted enough, the following night. I was truly on the point of abandoning all.

But then, early today, everything was altered – and in a way that would have made you laugh indeed. You told me when I was quite a child, I remember, about the mission stations' stores. How, although the missions do no trading, they nevertheless keep stores where the 'books', with which they pay their native helpers and with which they buy what they need when they go a-journeying, can be redeemed. I do not know that you ever told me that you had spent a morning inside one of these stores. But, passing the one here today, I took a fancy to go in, attracted by the bustle I heard.

What a sight met my eyes!

There was my frightening, fervent Père Jossuet, whose passionate warnings of the spiritual danger of the Forest were yet ringing in my ears, harassed to exasperation, poor man, by the clamour and demands of his 'customers'. No sooner had one great, half-naked fellow determined he wished to exchange his 'book' for half a dozen fish-hooks and one bright-spotted pocket handkerchief than of a sudden he would be seized by the charms of a box of lucifer matches and a hair-comb, established as being of the same value. But not for him a quiet request for a civilised exchange, which the worthy Père Jossuet, who cares for none of these things, would have been happy to effect. No, our matches and comb-loving friend must needs first proclaim, in a voice if possible louder than any of his neighbours', his feelings of woe at finding in his hands that fearfully despised pocket handkerchief, which not two minutes earlier had been the sole object of his desire. Then, lamentation done, it becomes of the first importance to him to effect an exchange instantly, to the discomfort and loudly expressed chagrin of all his fellows simultaneously bent upon exchanging pocket handkerchiefs for pomatum, pomatum for fish-hooks, fish-hooks for heaven knows what else.

Then, as well, the poor 'salesman' behind the counter has to keep a sharp eye on those others of his customers who are intent, in their fresh and innocent way, on abstracting any small article that touches their fancy and, under cover of the general pandemonium, tucking it under armpit or between legs and, if they remember its existence long enough, making their way outside with it, delightfully half-concealed in this manner.

So, as you can see, I found my stern monitor of the day before yesterday reduced to such haplessness that I was constrained to proffer my assistance. And I may say I acquitted myself not ignobly as a store-keeper. Happily, in doing so, I was able once again to see my intention of penetrating to the depths of the Forest, whence so many of these innocent fellows so harassing the good Father come, as a reasonable undertaking. No doubt the danger Père Jossuet spoke of is real. But it is, surely, no more than a danger. One that I must overcome as I may, should it be my ill-luck to be faced with it.

CHAPTER 3

Thomasina's pirogue took her slowly further upstream, long mile after long mile added to her already long tally. She sat half-reclining, against her stout box of trade goods. In Doctor Diver's notes there had been the observation that being provided with a store of such things as thin brass bars, penny-a-quart glass beads, fish-hooks and tobacco acted as a sort of passport of respectability for anyone travelling in Africa for such obscure purposes as botanising and entomologising. Like all the remarks in her mentor's notes it was one she had taken heed of.

As I looked beyond the box containing my supply of trade goods, in a mound that seemed to threaten the tree-trunk canoe's very stability, there were heaped the paddlers' sleeping mats, hard pillows and mosquito bars, together with their rations of plantains. My own long sausage-like waterproof bag, stuffed with spare clothes, my memoranda books and reading matter, with tea in many sealed packets and a large flask of Conde's Antiseptic Fluid, added to the general precariousness.

And, most precious of all, there were my Wardian cases, collapsed and wadded in straw. In them, one day, God willing, I will have secured, still growing, the clover-leaved plants from the swamp patch under the little, thrice-divided waterfall. Plants which, had Doctor Diver succeeded in bringing his specimen to England, would have perhaps brought relief and cure to my mild-mannered mother before those appalling oaths, words I would not have conceived possible to form any part of her vocabulary, had broken from the depths of her mind. The cure might, too, have prolonged for some last happy years my secret friend's own life, taken from him at a time when I had not been able once to leave my mother's bedside to soothe, in so far as I could, his equal agonies. If all went well, however, that cure would yet free countless thousands from the typhoid fever with its raging horrors that could stalk unchecked from the lowest reaches of society to the highest.

In front of me there were my paddlers. And I am obliged to acknowledge that, watching their broad, muscled, oil-gleaming backs as they bent to their work and hearing the deep-throated, vibrant, repetitive chants that seemed to well up from them without conscious effort, I was feeling a stirring of excitement that ran altogether counter to the serious intent of my quest. There was life, vitality, a go-anywhere willingness, a care-discarded cheerfulness in the fellows that spoke to me with an altogether new, unexpected, promise-hinted note.

To either side, across the mile-wide Congo, yet richer in its promise of an unknown, inexperienced, pulse-racing enjoyment, lay the Forest.

A scene I had thought on my first day on the great swift-flowing river, that might have come from antediluvian times. But now here it was, for me, unchanged. The timeless growth rising high from the river's very edge so that there was no saying where water ended and land began. Cliff-curtains of utterly dense green, as alluring as the curtain of the Salisbury theatre when as a child I had sat in the heart-beating expectation of witnessing marvels with its rise.

Sometimes the headman steering at her craft's almost blunt bow had changed course, perhaps to round a sullen sandbank or to keep well clear of the dark humps of bathing hippopotamuses or for inexplicable reasons not unconnected she suspected with juju. Then they had come close to one bank or the other, and there she had seen tangled networks of huge twisted roots rising from the mud. In front of these there might stand tall nenuphars, stems writhing up out of the water, waving wide, rich flowers, pink or yellow or virgin white. Looking up, she had seen the tops of huge trees, their great boughs – cathedral spans – arching out over the water, seeming to glide backwards above her as she reclined there.

Then, across the still, carved green cliff-curtain there might dart birds, colourful beyond any English countryside kingfishers. While from just inside the precipice-growths came their calls in chaotic variety, hoots, whistles, trills, water-gurglings, wood-sawings, screams as of a child in fright or a midnight banshee, squawks harsh and forbidding. Or, suddenly a wild chase of monkeys might appear out of the verdant cliff-face, swooping from branch to branch, creeper to creeper, and as suddenly disappearing into the deep within.

At every moment, it had seemed, there was some new sight to see. A new shape of leaf, a new tree, a new blossom would confront me which I must try to allocate a place in my mind. But the task soon proved beyond me. I accept that there dwells in the Forest confusion beyond cataloguing. This confusion, it now appears to me, will be with me until I attain the object of my quest. It would end only when I have wrested Doctor Diver's healing plant – should that ever come to pass – from its swampy hiding-place and have made my way back to England and its simplicities once more.

The swift current of the huge river slowly yielded to her paddlers' strokes, water of a shade almost exactly that of the tea in the cups at her mother's table in the house in the Close. Tea taken at precisely nine o'clock each evening. The memory came back to her of those long, quiet, ordered times. Of herself sitting reading. Of herself at the piano, playing (not really very well) a sonata by Benedict or Thalberg or singing 'The Captive Knight', the Canon's mildly romantic favourite. Of her needle threading in and out of her work in calm monotony.

And here, not so many months after those days had come to their sudden, shocking termination, here she was.

Here in a narrow tilting craft with half a dozen wild black men, under a sun that seemed an altogether different source of heat from even the brightest sun of an English summer. Here she was, sweat breaking from every pore, past all wiping away by no matter how many cologne-soaked handkerchiefs. Here, acutely uncomfortable, perfectly happy. Happy as, despite every setback, she had been at every moment of the long, long river journey.

I went to bed last night in the insect-full but pleasantly large hut which the chief of the village had hospitably put at my disposal, believing that at dawn today my faithful crew would be ready to set paddle to water once more. Yet at dawn they were nowhere to be found. So here I sit in the convenient shade of a tree, the name of which I have been unable to learn but for whose spreading branches and wide leaves I am profoundly grateful, and wait patiently for their return. That they will return I am perfectly convinced. This is not the first occasion some whim, or some important ceremony of juju they had innocently forgotten to give me warning of, has caused them to disappear into the Forest depths. There, as yet, I do not feel prepared to follow, were I even sure I could successfully do so. The Forest appears to gather to itself whoever ventures more than a few yards – no, a few feet – into its green confusion, and there is no sighting of them until they shake off the thrall and come out of their own free will. So I wait, and despite the nagging urgency of my business in Africa I cannot but feel that there is a good deal to be said for such breaches of promise as I now experience. They relieve the mind of responsibilities which no amount of fretting can advance one inch. These cheerful fellows, who have paddled me so willingly for so many river miles, have a simple creed, I begin to comprehend. Why, they ask, or do not indeed need even to ask, why should Man, at one with the animals, burden himself with obligations as though he were a moral being singled out from all other creation? And I find, daughter of a Canon of Salisbury though I am, that their creed, here in Africa, does not seem altogether anathema. Yet I must not let such thoughts-

My fellows have appeared out of the Forest, like spirits materialising, though a great deal more capable, I am pleased to think, of urging a solid pirogue upstream. We voyage again.

Round the slow arc of the bend in the river there came into view the trading station that was the final object of Thomasina's long weeks on the water. Now she was in the last minutes of the first great stage of her journey, mile upon mile of Africa put behind her, as many more miles of virgin Forest yet to come.

On the little leaning landing-stage ahead she could make out clearly now the figure of the trader. He was a tall, thin man, long legs encased in narrow striped-cotton trousers, a short jacket, almost white from repeated washings or repeated soakings in equatorial rain, unbuttoned across his chest. His face, which was adorned by a little goatee beard, was yellower than the jacket by many shades. Thomasina had seen enough of white men under the African sun to be able to put this strange hue down to a long course of fevers. She placed then in her mind this stranger, on whose hospitality she was about to throw herself, as a person of long experience in the Dark Continent.

Her craft neared the jetty. Her paddlers set up a new bright song and dug into the mud-swirling water with a will. The trader hailed them.

"By God, it's a lady."

The canoe bumped against the landing-stage. The headman seized one of the heavy log uprights and brought the craft, scraping and grinding, alongside.

The yellow-faced trader knelt with one knee on the rough boards and extended a hand, yellow as his face, to help Thomasina up.

"Forgive me, ma'am," he said, "if in the moment of my surprise I let out words I'd have better kept to myself. Jabez Sparrhawk at your service."

Thomasina recognised the peculiar accent with which he had spoken as American, though she had heard but one American speak before, at her hotel during one of her visits to London making her preparations.

"Miss Thomasina le Mesurier," she replied. "and I well realise that it must be more than a slight surprise to find a woman stepping out of a pirogue on to your landing-stage."

"Ma'am, it was, since you're good enough to say so. May I inquire what in tarnation - May I ask, that is, just why you're here?"

"Of course, sir. It is simple enough. I have come to Africa in search of a plant, a rare healing plant, discovered some twenty years ago by one Doctor Diver, an exploring botanist, now deceased. He - he was unable in the outcome to bring it back to the civilised world."

"Indeed, ma'am? But - well, I guess I'm constrained to ask: why are you, a lady, now going in search of this remarkable treasure?"

A spark of rebellion against such an unquestioning assumption of a certain order in the world sprang up in Thomasina.

"Is it not possible, sir, that a lady may be as well endowed with the qualities necessary for such an undertaking as a gentleman?"

"Why, no, ma'am, it ain't. Truthfully, I do not believe it."

"Yet, sir, since I have been in Africa I have seen native women bearing burdens their menfolk consider quite beyond them, and working harder by far in the fields and gardens than their lazybone husbands."

The trader seemed to blush a little under the yellow of his cheeks.

"You're certainly correct in your observations, miss," he said. "I confess that aspect of life in Africa had never particularly struck me until this moment. But - Well, you, ma'am, will be nevertheless a person, I suppose, who's been raised very differently from those women here bearing the heat and burden of the day, as the Good Book says."

"Yes, sir, yes," Thomasina answered, doing her best to conceal the flicker of doubt that she had begun to feel. "But I was not brought up in entire indolence. Ours was no pampered household. I was accustomed to take my share of its work."

Mr Sparrhawk looked down at her with an air of cool calculation.

"That may be so, ma'am. That may be so. But forgive a fellow who's spent more years than he cares to count under the African sun if he asks a question you may feel is a mite short in politeness. Put it down to Yankee manners, if you will. But such work as you were used to doing in old England, is that going to fit you truly for making your way through the Forest in Africa?"

Thomasina did not find it easy to answer immediately. The idea of her incapacity had, back at the time she had begun to put into reality the plan conceived in a single moment in the attorney's office in Salisbury, been strong in her mind. But she had subsequently immersed herself in such useful works as Francis Galton's Art *of Travel* and William Balfour Baikie's *Narrative of an Exploring Voyage* and had squarely confronted the difficulties and dangers they spoke of. She had read, too, the accounts of not a few lady travellers in scarcely-known regions of the world and of the women missionaries, and she had asked herself whether anything, in fact, prevented her doing as much as they had.

But, for all that in Africa until now she had found herself well capable of enduring what had to be endured and thrusting forward against such obstacles as had come her way, she still had inner doubts. She even, if she examined herself closely, retained a fear of the danger Père Jossuet had so burningly warned her against.

She was confident that she knew something of the Forest she was about to venture into. But, she knew too, that her knowledge was all too slight. She had had Doctor Diver's notes, of which she had made a careful synopsis during her weeks of preparation. But they had been generally more concerned with recording his botanical discoveries and with logging his mere position than with the actual hazards he had encountered. The other accounts she had read had, again, often not been so detailed as to give her any complete assurance about the vast confusion that awaited her.

"Mr Sparrhawk," she said eventually, "I can only tell you that I did not come to Africa wholly unprepared. Nor did I come without determination."

"And will that determination, ma'am, a woman's determination, serve to keep you pushing when you're shivering in a fit of fever? When maybe you've let jiggers get under your nails and they're hurting so much you think someone's putting a match-flame to them minute after minute?"

Thomasina bit the inside of her lower lip.

"I don't suppose I shall like that a bit," she said. "But I have visited the dentist and I did not like what he did, yet I saw it through."

The egg-yolk yellow eyes in Mr Sparrhawk's yellowed face glinted.

"I like your spirit, ma'am," he said. "Blessed if I don't. Yet is spirit going to be enough? I'm a plain man, ma'am, and I go by what I find. And I tell you this in plain friendship, no more: I've tramped my miles in the Forest, my hundreds of miles I guess, and I've traded for ivory and for rubber more years than I dare say you've been in the world, but I don't ever feel secure till I come out of there. And I can't see as how you'd be secure."

Thomasina lifted her chin as to take a blow.

"Then you are telling me that I am absurdly foolish to want to find a plant that will bring so much good to the world?" she said.

"No, ma'am, I'm not telling you you're foolish. I'm telling you you're plain foolhardy."

"But you believe I should go no further? That I should turn back?"

"Yes, ma'am, that's what I'm telling you. It's the truth as I see it."

"And if I reject your advice, well meant though I am sure it is?"

"Isn't that no more than a quick answer, right out of that spirit of yours? I like spirit in a woman. I like it in a man. In an animal even.

26

But spirit don't keep that man or that animal out of trouble."

Thomasina felt the tears move behind her eyes. She sucked in a breath to keep them back.

"Very well," she said, "if you will allow me to rest for the night here, I shall spend the time going over in my mind and in my conscience what you have said. Tomorrow I shall give you an answer. But I must warn you: I do not think it will be the answer you would wish to hear."

"I shall be happy to have you as my guest for just as long as you care to stay," Mr Sparrhawk replied. "And I shall await your answer with interest. No, with anxiety. True anxiety."

***

At the entrance to the bar a dwarf had come up to them, bandy-legged, an impudent grin on his deep chocolate-coloured face. A tray of mysterious miscellaneous objects hung from his neck. He challenged them in the local French that they were beginning to come to terms with.

"Gingembre, kola, autres aphrodisiaques?"

Tom dug her elbow into David's side.

"Doesn't need them, the randy sod," she said. "It must be Africa."

The dwarf seemed to understand the import, if not the English.

"Alors, vas-y, citoyen," he said to David, an immensely knowing grin on his jaw-jutting face.

The bar itself, when they went on into it, was a thumping confusion of noise and colour. The colour was among the dancers on the crammed and crowded floor, men and women in wrap-around bubus in every violent clashing shade. They shook, they moved, they gyrated, alive with rhythm and, unmistakably, with sexual charge. The noise came from the band up on its platform beneath a wide banner advertising Primus beer. A trumpet shrieked a high cascade. Four saxophones added a rich blast. And, louder than either, two sets of drums pounded and throbbed.

"Oh, yes," David shouted delightedly above the din. "Yes, yes, yes."

He put his head close to Tom's and roared against the thunderous rhythm,

"Like the beat-beat-beat of the Tom-Tom, when the jungle shadows fall, like the tick-tick-tock of the stately clock..."

"Yes, yes," Tom shouted back "I could take a fair amount of beat-beat-beat if this is the way things go every night."

"Then roll on delay. Which seems more than likely."

"Not a word. Not one word to remind me of that river-boat office. Oh, my God."

David naturally, launched at once into an imitation of the clerk they had spent the morning and afternoon arguing with, and with his timetables.

"Lisanga, Bomba, Basoko, Lokutu, Isangi, Pissangi, Kissangi, Blissangi. Oh, oui, citoyen, bateau va demain-demain."

"But not demain this semaine," Tom joined in.

"And d'you know – forget tomorrow, this week or next week - I think the great Steps *of a Jungle Gentlewoman* documentary may never get any further than the jungle we're in at this moment. "

"But it must. It will. If I have anything to do with it."

"Well, it mightn't be such a bad thing to go no further, all the same. We'd get some wonderful stuff in the native city here. All those lanes and alleyways with human life going on like crazy in them. Love and war. And music, and rows, and all the laughing faces. I love it."

"And what about B-J? Think he'd love the rushes? If we ever get any rushes to him, that is."

"To hell with B-J. We'd be giving him genuine off-the-map stuff. You saw the city-guide map. One great big blank two miles long where the native city is."

"And what about the government here? They going to hop up and down with delight when you plaster their buzzing old squalor all over the TV screens of the world? Remember the sayings of the great Boss on those poles all the way from the airport? *Be more alert, more thrifty, work harder so our beloved country becomes a model of organisation.* Wasn't that it?"

"Oh, I loved that. And all in English. Make sure no local understands. Good thinking, very good thinking. And you've forgotten the bit about the country having once been a *prototype of disorder*. I think prototype..."

He broke off.

"Oh, I say," he exclaimed. "Look at that."

Tom followed the direction of his gaze. It was clear what had caught his eye. *That* was a girl, revealed as the crowded dancers had moved a little apart. She was apparently dancing on her own, perhaps because, eyes more alight, teeth more flashing white, flesh more vigorously quivering, she had exhausted all her male partners. And she was altogether magnificent. Tall, full-bodied, with taut bouncing breasts, jutting buttocks, erect neck, wide-smiling rhythm-hypnotised mouth.

"Oh, God," David said, "I'm sorry, sweetheart, but I must have that. I must."

"Oh, thank you very much. Loyal lover. I really appreciate that."

David, already attempting to thrust himself into the hurly-burly of the dance floor, paused.

"I did lay my heart at your feet back home," he shouted over his shoulder. "Formal offer."

"But not on your knees. If you'd been on your knees you never know what I might have said."

"Oh, yeah?"

"And one thing more, David Teigh." Tom took a step nearer. "One thing more. Don't forget where you are. Africa. World epicentre of Aids, yes? It all began in good old no-holds-barred here. So don't come panting and slobbering into my bed if you get lucky with her."

David stopped and turned.

"Oh, no," he said. "Do you have to spoil it? Just when a never-to-be-forgotten frolic was there before me?"

"Not me that spoilt it, lover boy. Just wiggling little Human Immuno-suppressant Virus."

David stood irresolute. The magnificent creature dancing there seemed to have guessed his intentions. The extra wide smile she flashed was directed at him, beyond doubt.

"Oh, God," he said. "It would have been bliss. Unthinkable paradise."

"Just fun and games." Tom said.

"But not just that," he said. "Surely there must be the paradisal bit. There must."

"Yes? But the Big Guy in the sky put the snake into paradise, remember. He didn't call it Serpenticus Aidsiosus when he wrote the book, but it's there all right. It's there.

CHAPTER 4

At the edge of the clearing round Mr Sparrhawk's trading-station the Forest grew, bafflingly dense as it had been in the towering green cliffs along the wide Congo. Already, though it had been only a few weeks since the American trader had had the ground burned back, vegetation had begun to re-assert its claim. Tendrils snaked out across the still blackened earth. Young trees, rising eagerly to the light Mr Sparrhawk's workers had created, were thrusting skywards with almost visible speed. Lianas had swarmed upwards from branch to branch equally rapidly, their curling ends waving out into the clearing seeking hold wherever it was to be found.

Thomasina stood looking for a way to get into the frenzied green tangle. At her back there waited the three bearers Mr Sparrhawk had recruited for her in the week since she had told him that she had not, despite all his advice, altered her intention of making her way through the Forest.

Confronting the entangled mass, the thought struck her that she might actually be defeated by the impenetrable Forest before she had even set out. A flush of hot dismay rose up.

How Mr Sparrhawk would laugh. Or, no, he was too innately polite to laugh to her face. But it could hardly be expected of any mortal man not to feel a quiver of amusement at such a swift ending to such high aspirations.

But her aspirations were not so easily to be deflated. They must not be. Doctor Diver had reached that swamp patch beneath the little triple waterfall. This much was clearly stated in his oft read notes. It was not an impossible enterprise. She, in her turn, would accomplish it. She must accomplish it.

Yet, though considerately keeping to the far, river-facing side of the trading-post, Mr Sparrhawk was to all intents and purposes there at her elbow. She must set forth.

Her bag with her most necessary possessions in hand, compass, memoranda book, handkerchiefs, Warbury's fever drops, Mr Darwin's *On the* Origin *of Species* her specific against solitude, underlinen, her sturdy knife and, buried deep and waterproof-wrapped, the revolver she had little intention of using, she made a dart forward. She parted a thick grass clump almost twice her height, thinking that here might be the most vulnerable point in the tangled growth in front of her. She placed a firm foot in the gap she had thus created.

And a snake went hissing away within an inch of her boot.

She was unable to prevent a choked squeal leaving her throat.

Had Mr Sparrhawk heard?

It seemed not. No suppressed grunt of laughter came from the far side of the house.

M'bene, the leader of her little party of bearers, stepped past her, doing nothing to conceal the wide grin on his face. Yet Thomasina found it easy to forgive him, much easier than to forgive the smile she had not as much as seen on Mr Sparrhawk's yellowy countenance. She had taken to M'bene from the first moment she had seen him. She had insisted, against she was sure Mr Sparrhawk's judgment, that he be made the leader of her party. She liked at once his frank and immediate smile. She had rapidly found it possible to set aside the boastfulness that proclaimed itself in his manner and in the rudimentary French they shared. She felt his willingness to throw himself entirely into a new departure answered to something in her nature that in quiet, ordered England had been long suppressed. And she fought back the trickle of doubt the fellow's unchecked readiness had also set up in her.

In any case, she felt, she knew too little to make any final judgment about any African. Mr Sparrhawk had, in the course of giving her a great deal of considered advice, laid particular emphasis on what he had declared to be a gulf of difference between the white man and the African. Africans, he had stated, possessed as little sense of moral turpitude as if that quality had never been invented. But, expect nothing in the moral line, and you could trust an African in perfect safety. They might eat each other, but they would not offer to eat you. A white man – or a white woman – came, he thought, from too different a world to be considered 'a pretty item of diet.'

Thomasina had given the lanky American her full attention as, striding up and down the length of the trading-post veranda, he had unburdened himself of such thoughts for her benefit. He had, she decided, for all that he made no pretension to possessing a great deal of education, given deep consideration as he had tramped his hundreds of miles through Africa to whatever had come to his notice. His garnered wisdom was to be cherished.

Lying awake at night under the drapery depending from her mosquito bar, she had subjected what he had said by day to the full play of her mind. What in the end had particularly struck her was his dictum, several times repeated, of the need when occasion arose to be ready 'to think black'. The notion was both something novel to her experience and something she felt she should strive to acquire. If one could learn the trick of it, Mr Sparrhawk had said, one could 'get along tolerably well with a species of humanity as far removed from ourselves as is the moon above from the earth beneath.'

Yet what exactly the nature of this mind was that 'thought black' Mr Sparrhawk had found difficult to explain.

"I guess, ma'am, there ain't no words to put it into," he had said one evening at just that hour of the quick dusk before he had his lamps lit. 'It's a thing that don't fit into words. Africans go by something I've come to style feelings-thought. While you and I, my dear, go, like the rest of white humanity, decently by logic-thought. That's the difference. But I reckon till you've had feelings-thoughts you can't know what they are. And when you've had 'em you know what they are, quick though they be to fly out of a mind that never was intended, as a white mind, to have any such things inside it."

But now, with that seemingly impenetrable Forest wall in front of her, her trust in M'bene, with presumably his black thinking actively at work, proved justified. He simply went some seven or eight yards further along the dense tumult of vegetation and, despite his head

33

being encumbered with her long waterproof bag resting on it, slipped between the trunks of two thrusting young trees.

And revealed to her a path.

It was not much of a path. At home, she thought, she would not have regarded it as a path at all. There it would have been no more than the worn track made by some animal, sheep or even rabbits. Yet, following it behind M'bene's broad back, she was able to make her way into the Forest with only moderate difficulty.

As she advanced, she had to stoop, to twist, to step sideways as the tree-trunks and the manifold creepers dangling in the way dictated. But she had begun to make progress. If it was not as fast a pace as she was accustomed to on the mildest English stroll, it was a pace of sorts.

So, she thought, I am truly inside it now. Inside the great Forest that I have heard tell of since the first day I met dear Doctor Diver, kindest of men and most distrusted of savants by those panjandrums of science in their learned libraries in London. What the Doctor had told her of the Forest, its dangers and its delights, once no more than stories to please a childish acquaintance, later as thoughtful answers to her considered curiosity, was now becoming reality.

Her quest had moved into its final and proper phase. All that lay between her now and that swamp patch under the rock-divided waterfall was this selfsame Forest. Miles there were of it, lying ahead. Days and days of walking. Days that would see – she had already come to realise – often very few of those miles conquered. But she was in the Forest at last. In it, and moving through it.

All she had to do hereafter was to push onwards as best she might. No doubt things altogether unexpected lay ahead. From all she had learnt, from Doctor Diver, from William Balfour Baikie's Narrative, from talk aboard the trading vessel making her laborious way from Liverpool to the Coast, from tales that trader and missionary had told her here in Africa, from Mr Sparrhawk's earnest advice, she knew the Forest was unpredictability itself. But she was ready for even the most unpredictable of occurrences.

It was after another fruitless battle with the clerks at the river-boat company that, wandering through the Grand Marche with its football-stadium jabber of laughter-laced voices, David quite suddenly came to a halt. He took Tom by her arm.

"Let's have a drink," he said. "There's a bar over there."

Tom looked in the direction he had indicated.

"Oh, come on," she said. "You can't be needing a drink that badly. That place is grotty beyond belief. It's not all that far back to the hotel, you know."

"No," David said, with a jerk of obstinacy. "I rather fancy going there."

He gave a little puzzled frown.

"Don't know why," he said. "But I do."

The place was even less attractive than Tom had said, despite its name, Bar Vatican, painted in splashy faded lettering on a bare board outside. It was a single tin-roofed room with leaning folding doors at its front pushed open to their full extent. There were no more than half a dozen wooden tables inside, most of them slanting dangerously one way or the other. At the rear there was a counter covered in dull beaten zinc with behind it a couple of shelves displaying a few fly-blown bottles. On the blue-painted concrete walls hung two or three posters, advertising events long forgotten.

There were no other customers, and Tom insisted that at least they choose a table near the open. The proprietor, a lumbering fellow in greasy khaki pants and a once-white vest with a big hole in its front showing an expanse of black belly, came over and asked in a surly, hardly comprehensible French what they wanted.

"One Primus."

David turned to Tom.

"You too?"

"No. Whisky. Whisky neat."

"Pas de whisky. Y'a absinthe."

"Oh God. The cloudy yellow then, if there's mineral water. In a bottle."

"Alors, un Primus, une absinthe."

They watched, with anxiety, their orders poured at the zinc counter. The glasses, however, looked only a little smeared, and the drink came straight from the bottles.

Then, when they turned away to look out at the boisterous liveliness of the market, they found there was an ancient black man sitting composedly at the third chair round their table.

He looked as old as Africa itself. His face was a deep ruby colour and so criss-crossed with wrinkles that it resembled something like a tufted pincushion. The arms that hung from the colour-drained pinkish singlet he wore were fleshless and stringy. A scant grey layer of crinkled hair still clung to his head.

David took him for a beggar.

"No, no, not today, my fine fellow," he said.

"Oh don't be so pompous," Tom intervened.

Undeterred the old man retorted "vous êtes venus," in a French that was remarkably clear.

"Oh, yes, we've come," David answered. "We've come to your beautiful city, and it looks as if we've come to stay for ever. So..."

Again he gestured the old man away.

"I knew you would come. I directed you to this place. It is necessary that we talk. There is much to say."

David gave Tom a glance of puzzlement. She pouted a silent baffled reply and tackled their unwelcome visitor in her reasonable French..

"Look, you may have much to say but we do not want to hear it. We are not here to buy. We just want a quiet drink. I'm not sure why."

"No. You are wanting much more. You are wanting a boat that will take you up the great river."

David sat back in surprise both at the assertion and his own understanding the French being spoken to him.

"Saw us somewhere outside that awful office," Tom shot at him in English. "Followed us, saw us come in here, swooped. Simple."

"Yes," said the old man, who clearly had made no attempt to grasp Tom's rapid explanation. "Yes, you have been to the bureau. But I was not there, as perhaps you have supposed. I only saw you in there. Today, yesterday and the day before. You had much trouble."

"There needs no ghost come from the grave to tell us that," Tom, flicked out. "Trouble lies in wait in that place whoever you are."

"But I can tell you," the old man went on, ignoring the buzz of incomprehensible English, "your boat will be here in three days. I have seen it coming down the river."

"Three days away," Tom said, reverting to French, "You must have magnificent eyes, mon vieux."

"Ah, but it is not with these old eyes I see. I have better ways of seeing than that, and I tell you I have seen that boat."

The eyes in the old man's criss-crossed, ruby-coloured face were, in fact, so bleary and bloodshot it was not difficult to believe he could hardly see with them. David looked away.

"Well, I hope you're right, old son," feeling a vague uneasiness.

"You are saying that you hope? But I tell you, you will have what you desire. Your boat will come in three days. It will depart in five."

"Well," Tom put in, "that's certainly not the information we had. The boat is fourteen days late, so far as we could tell."

"And you will take N'goi with you," the old man answered, unperturbed by Tom's contradiction. "There will be much danger, and without him you will perish."

"Perish, eh?" David said, regaining with an effort his customary cheeriness. "But this is modern times, you know. There's antibiotics now. Insect repellents, even sunburn cream."

"Ah m'sieur, you joke. You joke very much. But, I tell you, you will not always joke in the Forest."

"Let that be a warning to you, David Teigh," Tom flipped in. "Less frivolity, more filming."

"Just let me get to that old primeval whatsit, and I'll see to the filming."

He stopped abruptly and turned to old N'goi.

"Wait a minute. Comment est-ce que vous savez que nous avez l'intention d'entrer dans la Foret?"

"Oh, come on," Tom broke in. "antibiotics, insect repellents. Pretty obvious really."

"Well, not all that obvious. I mean, you're going to need insect stuff wherever you are in this benighted place. And antibiotics are only a sensible precaution anywhere, too. Surprisingly sensible for us. But he's not to know that, our mysterious friend."

Tom shrugged.

"All the same," she said, "there could be dozens of ways he could have worked it out. And he may understand a bit of English, however little it looks like it."

"No", N'goi said, solemnly shaking his grey-grizzled head, 'you will need my counsel when you go into the Forest beyond doubt. Where you come from perhaps you know everything. But in the Forest you will know nothing."

"Ah," David pounced, "that's where you're wrong, mon vieux. What you haven't seen with your telescopic eye is our Major – what's his name, Tom?"

"Yombton-Smith. How could you forget?"

"Yes, my old N'goi. We've got the Yombton-Smith card to play when we get to the Forest. And I expect he'll be an ace. With a name like that how could he not be an expert explorer?"

"So," Tom said, leaning towards N'goi, "your advice was kindly meant, but it will not actually be needed. So can we buy you a drink before we go?"

"N'goi does not drink your foreign drink. And I do not think that any man who was not born in the Forest can understand its ways."

"You know, " David said in an aside to Tom, "I'm actually fairly impressed with our friend here. I mean, there may be something in what the old bugger says about the Forest, Yombton-whatsit or no Yombton-whatsit. After all, look what happened to Thomasina there."

"Okay, so she got into all sorts of trouble. But that was more than a hundred years ago, and she didn't really know all that much about rainforest conditions. And she was a lady all on her own."

"Yeah, but- well, I don't suppose the Forest's changed all that much, not the bits that haven't been chopped down. And there's still plenty of them."

He turned to N'goi.

"How much would you want to come with us, as – as, shall we say technical adviser?"

"M'sieu, I am coming with you. But I will come as your cook. You will need a cook. And I will come for a cook's pay only."

David turned to Tom again.

"Now, that's more than impressive. I don't mean the *je vais venir* bit. I'm just not going to think about that. But being ready to come for a cook's pay is good solid stuff."

"Well, I can see what you mean. But all the same I'm not at all sure."

"No? Well, I think actually the mumbo-jumbo's pretty convincing as well. This is Africa, after all."

"Oh, Teigh. The Dark Continent? Really."

"No, I reserve judgment on that. I really do. There are more things in whatsit and where than are dreamt of in your philosophy, old Potato."

"Okay then, okay. Provided he sticks to his side of the bargain. Strictly cooking, and cook's pay."

David turned again to N'goi.

"Right. Perhaps we will take you. If we ever set eyes on that boat, that is."

"Your boat will come. In three days. It will leave after two days more. I will be there."

***

Soon Thomasina began to acquire the knack of Forest travel. Much of the time she had to watch each step she took, to avoid a tree root, a sudden squashy declivity, an entangling creeper. But every now and again in those first hours she was able to lift up her eyes and look about her.

What had struck her most forcefully as they had penetrated into the deeper, more open Forest, though Doctor Diver had spoken of it often enough, was the coolness and the gloom, the green gloom. Fierce, she knew, though the sun was overhead, it was hardly capable of penetrating the layer after layer of leaves between ground and sky. Only when she halted and peered upwards could she see peepholes of intense blue. And they, she thought, must be a full two hundred feet above her, almost half as high as the tip of the great, calm spire of Salisbury Cathedral that had dominated her days from her very earliest memories. The quantity of leaves between herself and the sight of those tiny blue patches defied all calculation. Of every shape and size, of all possible shades of green, they lay still as if they were painted there, wave after wave of them, a whole new high hung world.

And up to them went the trunks of the trees, rounded and immense, almost white in colour often, springing for the most part from giant buttress-like ribs, ten feet or more in height. While snaking up, up, up, right to the underside of the high leafy ocean above, ran the lianas, thick sometimes as her own body, thin elsewhere as the indelible pencils in the bag at her side, twisting, tangling, swooping, trailing. Nor, down in the green gloom through which they were making their way, was there any colour. Here, far below where the sun shone, no flowers opened to its rays. No birds sang.

Under her feet as she followed M'bene there grew almost nothing. There was only the thick spongy weft and warp of debris, fallen leaves, twigs, insect bodies, the thin crushed skeletons of birds and rodents, dead branches, often disintegrating at a touch and giving off a new puff of the odour of decay that was everywhere, sharp and almost metallic.

She thought of all the years, the centuries, that must have gone to the making of this mush of decomposition. Of the slow life of the Forest, descending tiny piece by tiny piece all around her. Of the leaves in the mighty trees above, unfolding, thickening, greening, then yellowing and at last falling, their place taken by newly-unfolding leaf itself all too soon to fade and fall and add itself to the black cushiony layer over which she was now marching.

***

Ancient N'goi's prophecy curiously impressive in their ears, David and Tom left the Bar Vatican for the hurly-burly of the huge market once more. Dazzled and delighted, they walked past arrays of brilliantly-coloured cotton prints draped from the bars of stall after stall, each presided over by a wobblingly fat mammy, herself clad in cloth as vibrant as any of the lengths she was selling. And selling they were, each and every one of them. They shouted at the passers-by, insult and gross compliment. They seized hold of any pretty young girl who came within reach, hauled her in front of their wares, talked, laughed, cajoled. Other stalls were as gaudily chaotic, awash with socks or suspenders or handkerchiefs or head-scarves in pulsating clashing colours.

Then there were grocery stalls, a new great area of competitive yelling. Palm-oil in bottles of every shape, size and colour, begged, borrowed or stolen from heaven knows where, jostling each other in packed sun-glinting arrays. Great mounds of manioc, in its original knobby roots, in banana-leaf rolls of the pounded stuff, in huge brilliantly white powder heaps, clamoured for attention. Fruits and vegetables in every colour, in every twisted shape were hawked and cried. Bananas, green and yellow, huge or tiny. Pairs of sorghum spikes on their hairy stalks. Piquant pilipili in piles and heaps of startling red. Papayas, green and spiny. Coconuts, kola nuts.

Next, meat of every sort, high-smelling, fly-buzzing. Drawn-out strips of blood-bright beef. Bulbous mounds of offal, greyish, purply, yellowy. And the blackened shiny smoked carcases of monkey, porcupine, crocodile, okapi, lizard and snake, produce of the illimitable Forest stretching away from the jam-packed steamy city. With, beside them, yet odder products of the Forest riches, little oily spoonfuls of fried flying ants on torn pieces of newspaper, basins of hairy orange caterpillars, eyes protuberant, wriggling, wriggling. Sacks of damp earth keeping moist the sprawls of fat white grubs.

Looking down at them, David's broad face contorted in an involuntary grimace of dismay.

"All the same," he said, "I like this. I love it. I love it all. I'm even delighted with that awful creep in the bar just now. Old N'goi. Old N'goi."

"Yeah, well, I have my doubts there," Tom said. "I mean, second sight or whatever it is? I can't really go a bundle on that. And I'm not too sure about this place either. All right, it's exciting, here and everywhere else in the city. It's relaxed. Life's easy. It's got fizz. But are we ever going to get out of it?"

"Votre bateau va arrivé en trois jours," David said in a fair imitation of N'goi's lucid but faintly thick French. "But it's not only old N'goi I rather care for myself. It's everybody in the place, black or white."

"Well, yes. They're nice and - what's that they keep on saying we must be? Décontracté? Yes. Sois décontracté. They're relaxed all right. But all the same..."

"No, it's more than that really. It's - well, this is a place where everybody can be themselves. It's no-holds-barred land. All the rules have sort of slipped away. I mean, in some ways it's pretty ghastly, poverty-stricken, tatty, you name it. Those rusty old cranes all along the river, doing nothing almost all the time, far as I can see. The big dream of western progress and order they tried to clamp down on messy old Africa, all pretty well gone to seed... And, yet..."

"Yet? Yet? Come on, what yet? Horny old Teigh having his way with dozens of luscious African chicks?"

"I like that," David replied in mock outrage. "Who stopped horny old Teigh the other night? Tough old Tom, that's who. And, in any case, that's not what I was getting at. I meant it's the people we've talked to. All right, some of them are fearful white misfits, I admit. But even those ones are doing their own thing. And there are others just as extraordinary. Think of that great big drunk, Zairean expert on ancient African customs. Others, too. All of them go around being the people they actually are. Bad or good or indifferent. God, you could go half a year in London without meeting a quarter as many genuine, off-the-wall, head-in-the-clouds eccentrics as we've bumped into here in a couple of weeks."

"And you're all ready to become one of them yourself, David Teigh?"

"Am I?"

David stopped and wondered. The proprietor of a stall selling plastic watch-straps and ballpoints in long laid-out rows tried to thrust a particularly repulsive pink strap at him, poking it up towards his face. He ignored it.

"Ready to become one of them?" he said. "Should I be? I don't know. I'm not sure. But I tell you this much: this is where I feel I'm at least in danger of catching the fever. Unpredicabilityitis, severe attack of. Very good thing to have, I suspect. And none of these antibiotics you insisted we brought will cure it either."

Tom looked at him.

"Well, I hope to God your old N'goi's right about that bateau," she said. "Because I'm going to have to get you out of here fast and into that Forest if I ever want to be filmed as Tom Mountjoy discovering the hidden diaries of Thomasina le Mesurier.

CHAPTER 5

M'bene had killed a snake. It had been, Thomasina was well aware, an appallingly rash act. The snake, hanging red-brown, yellow-patterned from the branch of a tree right over their path, had been immediately recognised by all three of her bearers. It was, they had cried out, 'ompenle.' And she had heard much of the ompenle. It was, she had been told again and again, the only snake against the bite of which there was no remedy. So, beautiful though at any other time she might have found it, looping down, broad almost as a man's thigh, three feet or more in length and curiously velvety in appearance, she had felt overcome by all the old detestation of slithering things she had begun to shed in her days in the Forest.

Snail-Shell, the oldest and most cautious of her bearers – so called by her because she had not been able, back at Mr Sparrhawk's trading-post, to get her tongue round his proper name, and he had, besides his slow ways, a Snail-Shell talisman conveniently dangling from his neck – had at once stated it would be necessary for them all to go back until they could find a certain liana that resembled the ompenle. Then, when they had pretended to kill that in the prescribed manner, they would find their path clear once more.

But they had all been almost dropping with fatigue. For three days they had found no game of any sort to eat and precious few edible roots. So M'bene had brusquely ignored his senior's advice. He had loosened the machete he carried from the twined-creeper belt at his waist, and, crouching a little, had advanced on the dangling, red-brown, yellow-patterned shape. Nor had his advance, as even Thomasina knew it should be, been stealthy as he could make it. Recklessness sharpened by hunger, he had gone towards the ompenle more heavy footed, she had thought, than she had ever heard him.

The ompenle, of course, had been alerted. Thomasina had seen its little diamond-eyes glitter in the Forest gloom. It had stiffened upwards from its hold on the branch.

She wanted to call out. To order M'bene to stop. But any sound from behind, she feared, would only have served to distract him. And if then the ompenle struck...

She had forced herself to keep still, to keep as still as the unmoving foliage behind her.

But as the red-brown snake had made its dart towards M'bene he had swung his machete. It had been a wild blow. And a lucky one. The tip of the machete had creased the ompenle just beneath its darting-tongued head. For a moment its lunge had appeared unchecked. But then, almost on the point, it had seemed, of reaching M'bene's neck with its venomous fangs it had suddenly sagged. Its hold on the branch above had loosened. It had fallen and lain writhing on the path for a moment or two. Then it had been plain that it was dead.

M'bene turned towards them, eyes alight with triumph.

"Fool," Snail-Shell barked.

But M'bene was past being rebuked.

"If you do not want to eat," he said, "do not eat."

Snail-Shell glowered at him. But without another word, he began to hunt about for wood for a fire.

Thomasina watched the three of them, M'bene, Snail-Shell and the youngest of the party, a lad from a distant, different tribe nearer to her eventual destination, called Fito, almost always silent, always with a smile just not breaking through on his smoothly youthful face. In no time they were squatting by the fire, eagerness all over them, each holding a piece of the cut-up snake over the flames on the end of a sharpened stick.

She had never eaten snake, although two or three times before she had seen others do so. But that had been when she had had ample supplies of her own. In the past week, however, after they had found in their line of march a tributary of the mighty Congo with stretching back from its bank a whole tract of ten-foot tall sword-grass – rightly so named, cutting at a touch – and had been forced to make a long

45

wearisome detour she had gone increasingly hungry.

So now she found herself in a sharp dilemma. On the one hand, Stomach cried out insistently for sustenance, and the odour of the roasting snake was terribly appetising. On the other hand stood Civilisation – all she had ever heard, read or seen in pictures of the serpent tribe, from her mother's lips telling her the story of Adam's downfall to the occasional grass-snake encountered, alive and sinuous, in some quiet meadow on the outskirts of Salisbury. Schoolgirl epithets – You snake in the grass, you beastly viper – came back to her. And the tales told her, with grisly relish, in the boat on the way out.

Stomach won. She came forward to the fire, and M'bene at once offered her the piece of his victim that he had just finished cooking. She sank her teeth into it. It ate well. Better far, she thought, than the wretched fowls she had consumed in her first days on the Coast.

Refreshed, they made better progress and soon came to a place where the path widened out, and, without need for discussion now that the four of them knew each other as well as they did, the day's march was brought to an end. All too soon darkness would fall, sudden, almost as an extinguished lamp.

Snail-Shell began making another fire. M'bene slashed at a few still obtrusive saplings and vines, grinning enormously and re-enacting his triumph over the ompenle. Tall, silent, young Fito piled up their burdens in the way best calculated to preserve them from ants or sudden descents of rainwater from some high overhead leaf spilling its cupped contents.

Thomasina drew out her memoranda book from her bag while there was still light to see by. Twining a handkerchief round her wrist to absorb the sweat, she entered the number of miles she estimated they had travelled that day. They were pitifully few. Then, too overcome by fatigue to write more, she let the book fall shut and simply sat, sipping the tea that Snail-Shell had made for her, and gave herself over to contemplation of the state of things.

She was at least, she reflected, an experienced Forest traveller now. How much more so than on that distant morning when she had almost failed to enter the Forest at all, scared witless by the little snake she had almost trodden on. Now snake was settling comfortably in her stomach. Now, if she was nowhere near as clever as old Snail-Shell at spotting a bees' nest and raiding it for honey, she could at least be certain of recognising an itaba vine at the root of which good eating lay.

She could deal, too, with filaria worm. – Doctor Diver's notes had given her that scientific name – when with appalling speed it made its home under the skin. More than once she had, with a calmness she prided herself on, taken a splinter of wood, impaled the nasty thing with it and had slowly and carefully wound it out so that not a fragment remained to cause intolerably painful suppuration. There was an accomplishment to equal or even excel her mastery of Thalberg's sonatas.

She had traversed her miles and miles of Forest, in its varying ways and conditions. Sometimes descending into swampy stretches that had to be toilsomely waded through. Sometimes, where trees had fallen, becoming so dense with new growth as to be impenetrable. On occasion mysteriously full of huge beetles, large almost as soup-plates, or draped with immense spider-webs. Once, for two whole days, they had made their way through a pillared wonderland of tall trees, uniform in girth, uniform in their grey-white colour, mile upon mile. Then there had been areas where the lianas proliferated to an extent hard to believe, some hanging down for a hundred feet or more in lines straight as a brick-layer's plumb-cord, others coiled and coiled round each other till they formed gnarled cylinders thick as the trunks of the trees they depended from.

The Forest had become for her, day by day, a whole library. Riches, little by little, had been revealed. She had, she felt, perused now a goodly number of its volumes, read, marked, learnt and digested them. But, for each volume put back on the shelves, she had become aware of a dozen others untouched behind.

Her father, she thought suddenly, had once expressed the same notion to her. He had been talking of his days at Oxford as a Fellow of his college, before he had married. And he had said just that of the books in the Bodleian library. How, though he had read and read, it had always seemed there were as many volumes still to be perused in front of him as there were those assimilated behind him.

But the Forest library was more complicated, more abounding, more entangled than any collection of books, however massive. With books there was some hope of at last ending the cataloguing, however sadly behindhand the librarians might have got. But here in the Forest there was surely no hope of ever coming to a conclusion. There was too much of it to be encompassed by human understanding, not for however many years it was worked upon. And with each year, each month, each day, something new was being added. New books were being, as it were, written all around her at every moment. In new languages, in new forms of verse, transforming, re-creating, spreading.

Yes, though she had learnt a little, she was deep enmeshed in darkness still. In the dark uncanny. With a vision of books floating down on to her like so many light-winged, many-shaped, huge Forest moths she fell asleep.

***

They were all four of them, the Steps *of a Jungle Gentlewoman* crew, sitting at the bar of the hotel at the start of the evening. Boredom hovered over them like an invisible nerve-gas, waiting to descend.

"You did say it would be three days," perky Reg Blandy complained. "Well, it's three days now, and no sign of that boat. What exactly did they tell you at the riverboat office?"

"They didn't tell me a bloody thing," David snapped. "I just thought it would be about three days. I'm sorry. I'm sorry."

"They never tell you anything at that place," Tom put in, leaning back on her high stool. "Not unless an occasional murmur about a fortnight's delay is anything."

"Well, I understood it was definite about three days," Reg persisted. "I like to keep to schedule, you know. I just want to be clear when I'll be expected to start filming. So that I'm ready. It's not too much to ask. Is it, Josh?"

Josh Perkins, humped over a Primus beer under the blond thatch of his hair, started to life at the sharp sound of his name.

"Eh? What? What's that?"

"I said it's not much to ask, is it?"

"Um. Sorry. Not what? I was listening to the sound of this place. You know, it's nothing like as resonant as you'd expect, despite all those mirrors. I think it must be something to do with the humidity."

"Oh, Jesus," Reg said, "can't you ever take notice of what's going on around you? I was telling them: it isn't right us being given to understand we'd be off in three days and now nothing happening. I wrote to the missus, said we'd be out of touch from now on. And we're not."

"Oh, yes we are though," Tom said cheerfully. "Think. Have you had a single letter since we've been here? Of course, you haven't. And where do you think all those letters are that you write to your wife?"

"With her at Wimbledon, I should hope."

"Still in the post office here, I bet."

"But - but it's been weeks."

David broke in.

"Look, who's come."

They all turned, even Josh.

At the door way old N'goi had appeared. His ancient dried-up body in its drained pink singlet looked utterly incongruous in the would-be sophisticated ambience of the bar, with its engraved mirrors all round, its chrome and black PVC chairs. Yet the old man had no air of feeling himself out of place. Nor did either of the two waiters, smart in their short if dirtyish white jackets, make any move to chase him out.

After a moment he came padding bare-footedly over.

"The boat has come," he said.

"No, no, mon vieux," David replied. "You've got it wrong. You can see the smokestack of the boat from the veranda here, so they all tell us. And it isn't here. I went and looked just ten minutes ago."

"That is the riverboat," old N'goi answered. "But your boat is not that one. Your boat is here now."

David sat for a moment, then slid off his bar-stool.

"Hey," Tom said, "you're not actually going to look?"

"Well, yes. Yes, I think so. Somehow I get the feeling our friend here knows more than we do. And - and in any case a stroll down to the river won't do me any harm."

"Oh, Christ, then I'll come with you."

At the dockside they found – David had become increasingly confident they would find something – a cargo vessel that had just tied up. She was a large, smart-looking craft with a gleaming white raked superstructure aft and a long length of cargo deck in front. Stevedores were setting about unloading her, in a leisurely manner.

"There is the Capitaine," old N'goi said, pointing. "You must ask him for a passage, but he will agree."

David and Tom looked at each other, shrugged. David hailed the man N'goi had pointed out, a grossly fat individual in a white uniform, largely unbuttoned, standing flapping with an old cotton hat at his big bald head from which hung limp strands of long black hair.

"M'sieu le Capitaine? Is there any chance of you taking some passengers up river? A film crew? Four of us. Oh, and our cook here, too?"

"Why not? If you are ready to sleep on deck and can bring your own food. We leave in two days."

Again Tom and David looked at each other. Not only had old N'goi been right about 'your boat' coming in three days, but it now seemed he was right as well about it leaving with them in five.

"Well," David said, "a nice surprise for our famous Major Yombton-Brown after all."

"Yombton-Smith. Yombton-Smith. For God's sake get it right. If he gets huffy when we take him away from that scientific team he's looking after up there, B-J won't thank you. The arrangements cost him."

"Promise, promise. Yombton-Smith. Smith, Smith, Smith. And it's heigh-ho for the great exploring life."

"It's brace yourself for the Forest, buccaneer Teigh. And don't you forget it. I've a notion it's going to come as a big surprise to you."

The very plenitude and confusion that surrounds me on every side is, I find, my dear, good, dead friend, unexpectedly - what shall I say? Pleasurable? Fascinating? Heart-warming? I ought, I sometimes tell myself, to fight against this. I know as your disciple, my dear mentor, that I ought to be chronicling, ordering, categorising the multiplicity before me. When for a few moments at night by the dancing flames of our fire I read Mr Darwin's book – the very volume you gave me at my twenty-first birthday and which, like a schoolgirl with a novel supposedly too 'advanced' I kept in concealment – I make resolutions that the following day I will note at least one instance to confirm Mr Darwin's theory from my own observation. But, come daylight, come the tumultuous life all around, and my best resolutions wither into nothingness. The confusion, the chaos of it all, winds me in its delightful tendrils and I am powerless.

And I wonder now at this moment, accepting that Mr Darwin's belief is correct – how those words on my pen, or rather my indelible pencil, would have scandalised my poor, dear papa – accepting that the idea of the progress of creation is correct, then can it be perhaps that man is becoming, generation by generation, more able to accept chaos. In order to survive, is man becoming little by little a being who cheerfully embraces chaos? I find, certainly, that that is what I myself am inclined to do; and I wonder, too, if this feeling, this inclination, is what lies behind the mania for exploration that appears to have overtaken the civilised world these past fifty years? Are we, human beings, becoming more and more able to accept the unruly? Oh, my dear friend, how I should like to discuss this with you in your good, old, thorough manner. But, when we used to talk, how little I knew. How little, how very, very little I had thought.

In strict accordance with old N'goi's prophecy they left at dawn just two days after Tom and David had made their rapid bargain with the cargo-boat captain. The vaguely-seen outlines of the great empty dockside sheds and the tall idle cranes slipped by in the pearly-grey light. Dredgers, low in the water and listing as if they would never work again, loomed up, sank away. An abandoned paddle-steamer, the river sloshing in at its lower deck from their passing wake, was left forlornly behind.

"And this, too" David said, as he and Tom leant on the rail looking out, "has been one of the dark places of the earth."

"Très poetic. But what the hell do you mean?"

"Not me, love. Conrad. *Heart of Darkness*. Set precisely here. I did a heck of a lot of work on old Conrad when I was toying with my B. Litt. Knew that story practically by heart in those dear old swanning academic days."

"One of the dark places of the earth? I doubt if it's going to come up to that, all the same. I imagine like most of the places I've been to for Far Flung Films it'll all turn out to be pretty boring."

"But good old Tom Mountjoy, direct to camera, will nevertheless put over with shining enthusiasm a totally false picture."

"Well, no, not totally false. Just a bit jazzed up. After all, life's never as crammed with the new and unexpected as we'd like it to be."

"As you would like it to be. You and your faithful cohorts of couch potatoes."

"Come on, Teigh, you're hardly a confirmed keeper-to-the-track yourself."

"No, s'pose not. But, let me tell you, every now and again a distinct urge sweeps over me to give up the chop-and-change lark and really settle down."

"You're not proposing again, are you?"

Tom's wedge of a face seemed to be expressing real dismay, even a flicker of fear.

David saw it.

"Marriage an awfully big adventure?" he teased.

"Oh, God, if only it was. But I strongly suspect it's the very opposite."

"Well, don't worry, love. I was only just glancing at the possibilities. Of settling down, I mean. And I don't think your actual marriage is necessarily part of the package. I mean, for one thing I don't see that a piece of paper makes it any more definite, really."

"Glad to hear it," Tom said with a touch of wryness.

And then, quite suddenly, they were in the midst of a dense mist. Greyish and warm, wreaths and feathers of fog had moved up the sides of the boat, creeping and dabbing. In a few moments a thick layer lay on the surface of the deck. And, less than a minute later, they could see nothing.

The Capitaine, in the wheelhouse above, must have ordered the engines to a halt. With a suddenness that was in itself not unalarming the heavy throbbing that had become part of their surroundings died into silence.

"We're drifting, I think," David said.

"Yes, I suppose we would be. She'll have had some way on her. She's a pretty big craft."

"Do you - do you think we'll hit anything? Christ, some other boat. Anything."

"Nothing else near. Or at least there wasn't before the fog came up. This isn't the channel, you know, with cargo-ships squeezing by each other like people on the Oxford Street pavements and hovercraft buzzing to and fro every five minutes."

"No. No, I suppose not. But all the same... I mean, say we run into a sandbank or something."

"If we do, we do. After all, your beloved old N'goi only guaranteed we'd set off on the fifth day. He never said anything about arriving."

"Well, but, my God."

"Oh, relax. This is good. It's how things ought to be. Drifting, and not knowing where we are. It's exciting. And it's what life's really like, too."

"Philosophy. In the fucking fog. And, in any case, I'm not sure that is what life is like. I mean, I don't see why it shouldn't have at least some order in it."

"Christ, I believe you're sodding proposing once more. That's twice in an hour. And, besides, fog like this must happen often enough on the river. Our fat friend in the wheelhouse doesn't seem particularly worried."

"How do you know? You can't see the bugger, can you? Not in this. For all we know he may be throwing a thousand fits."

"But you've got ears, haven't you? I don't think M'sieu le Cap is actually bellowing with fear."

"Well, he bloody ought to be. That's all I can say."

"You know, Teigh, I don't think you're going to be as dynamic as

I thought on this trip. Not if you create like this at the first sign of things going wrong."

"It's not things going wrong... oh, well, yes, it is, in a way. It's that I do like to know what I'm doing, basically. I mean, all right, one doesn't want to live a sort of Reg Blandy life, strict railway lines from cradle to grave. But one does want at least to know more or less where one is at any given moment. And that, literally, is what we don't know now."

"Oh, yes, we do. We're in the Dark Continent. Remember?

CHAPTER 6

Reg Blandy, as if David's chance reference to him had summoned him up out of the fog, loomed into view.

"Did I hear my name mentioned?"

"Oh, Chri – er - hello, Reg. Won't be much for you to do, will there, not if we're going to have fog like this all the way up the river?"

"Oh, really, David," Tom said, joining in the rescue, "we're hardly likely to be wreathed in the mist for four solid days. I bet there isn't anything in - what's it - *Heart of Darkness* about the river being fogbound from end to end."

"No, there isn't," Reg Blandy chirped unexpectedly. "Jolly good yarn that. Read it years ago, of course. But I remember it. I was thinking of it when we set off actually."

"You're a Conrad fan, too, are you, Reg?" David said, still over-hearty. "Join the club."

"Oh, yes. I used to love adventure tales. In my young days. Before I sort of had adventures of my own. Eventually went as assistant to some pretty hot spots, you know."

"Did you indeed? I had no idea."

"No. Well, you wouldn't, would you? But before I married Mrs. Blandy and had commitments I was a regular rolling stone. Freelance. Grab any job that took me out of old G.B."

"So you came with us just to get away from old - from Britain?"

"Well, no, not really. I'd rather be at home with Mrs. B nowadays, if you get me. But there's the money aspect. We've just acquired a motor-home, and the instalments are killing. Killing."

"So you succumbed to the lavish offer B-J made you?" Tom put in.

"Well, I wouldn't say lavish. No. Not exactly. But work's hard to come by these days. So I had to take what Mr Brentiswood-Jones agreed to pay."

"You sound as if you'd rather be doing almost anything else," Tom joked.

"Well, I would. Within reason. I mean, this isn't an outfit that's run on proper lines, is it? I ought to have an assistant by rights. And a grip. It's all defying Union rules, you know."

"I know Reg, I know. But you know B-J too, don't you? Not a chap to take much notice of rules. Never has been. Doesn't really admit their existence."

"I'll say," David chimed in, repairing bridges yet again. "God, the only time I've ever been in a car with B-J... when I'd been down to his country place to fix this up, and he offered me a lift back to London. Jesus, I was scared."

"So was I, first time he ever drove me," Tom added. "I was more frightened then, I tell you, than on my first expedition when I was threatened with rape by a six-foot Afghan."

"Yeah. You know, I thought of B-J when we were flying out here and I was reading a Simenon book. He said something in it about *les gens qui n'avaient besoin des règles*. And I thought: B-J, B-J to a tee."

"I'm sorry," Reg Blandy said sharply. "What does that mean? We don't all speak French, you know."

In the grey gloom of the fog David blushed.

"I'm sorry. It's - it's - er - something about people who don't have any need for - er - rules."

"Oh, I see. Well, I can't understand that. I mean, you've got to have rules, haven't you? Otherwise where would anyone be?"

He gave them both a cock-robin glare.

"But I must go and check over my cameras," he said. "When this fog lifts there'll be some nice footage going. River scenes."

"Absolutely right, Reg," David said. "Just what we want. Typical Congo river scenes and voice-over from the earlier parts of Thomasina's diaries, like that sandbank bit if you remember."

"The river's called the Zaire now," Reg corrected him. "That's official. It's river Zaire scenes you want."

"Was the bloody Congo when Thomasina was writing that bit in the diary. You bald little pedant!" muttered David to the retreating figure of Reg Blandy.

Another whim of my sturdy paddlers. Another delay. Yet I can scarcely find it in me to blame them. Yesterday, as we made our way slowly up river, the headman suddenly gave a joyous cry, interrupting the steady singing. What had occasioned it was no more, to me, than the sight of a tall palm-frond standing up out of the water, though with all gracefulness. At once, however, we steered for the village that stood on the bank nearby, and it soon became evident that, though it was hardly past noon, our day's journeying was over. We spent the night in the village, amid the customary hospitality and discomforts. This morning the reason for the abandonment of our routine – so often and so easily abandoned in Africa – became apparent to me. That palm-frond had been posted where it was in order to measure the fall of the river and the emergence of a splendid sandbank. No sooner was this fully exposed than out to it in every canoe they could lay hands on went all the lads and lasses of the village. Needless to say, my pirogue was pressed into service, though it did also take out to this God-sent playground all my crew. Playground is the word, too. Hemmed in all year by the ominous Forest, what delight it must have been to have, for however short a time, a wide, unbroken stretch of land, or of sand, to frolic upon. So now before me there is a scene of uninhibited rejoicing. Merry brown forms dance or lie stretched on the golden-yellow strand. Gaudy patchwork quilts and equally gaudy chintz mosquito-bars lie airing in the sun, like so many giant butterflies of every hue under heaven. I have not been invited to the party. I suppose I am considered too grand. I wish it were otherwise. The whole affair radiates happiness. The African believes, with absolute conviction, I think, that the aim of life is happiness, happiness and pleasure. And, alas, in my heart I have to tell myself it is not so. Perhaps they knew best, after all, in not sending me a card.

When the fog lifted, quickly, inexplicably, and the Capitaine had ordered the engines to be started again David said "I remember now."

"Remember what?"

"Conrad. *Heart of Darkness*. He did have fog in it. Our Reg was wrong. It came down somewhere during that long river journey in the battling little boat with its leaking steam pipes. And, what's more, he said - listen to this, Tom, I can quote almost the exact words. The fog came back, he said, like a white shutter sliding down in greased grooves. Bloody good image."

"Well, so what?"

"So just watch out for our fog coming back any minute."

But the fog did not come back, and the big boat made steady progress up the wide river. Endlessly, it seemed, it chugged its way forward through the glassy sun-reflecting water. To either side, now distant, now nearer, the Forest stood implacable in unmoving cliffs of green. From time to time they skirted islands, immense dark-green basking sharks in the tea-brown water.

Round each slow bend the sight that met their eyes seemed unvarying. The glass-bright river pockmarked with little eddies, the distant shores enlivened now and again with an advancing army of tall grasses, feather-headed and hardly moving. Occasionally a white bird or two would fly lazily overhead. Great clumps of water-hyacinth, lilac-toned flowers rising up above, on thick stems , floated towards them, slid past, floated away again.

"You remember what that big Zairean ethnicity expert told us about those?" Tom said as an even larger clump, a floating island, slipped by.

"Whatever it was he must have been half-drunk at the time."

"No. I believed this. It's so typical of life."

"I'd agree. I'd agree absolutely. If I knew what you were talking about."

"Oh, come on, Teigh. He said that water-hyacinth – jacinthe d'eau, sounds more romantic – he said it had only got into the river in the late '50s. Some American missionary thought it would look nice in his garden, had some sent to him. But he hadn't reckoned with proliferating old Africa, and before he knew it the whole river was loused up with the stuff. You think you're just making a pretty little garden, and you find you've launched a menace to navigation."

"Ah, but that's where you're wrong, my sweet. I've been watching those clumps floating up to us, and, do you know, they ain't no menace to navigation. We're actually steering by them. They always take the fastest-flowing channel, which is the one that happens in this shifting, shifty old river to be the deepest at the moment. Pretty good, eh?"

But the clump that had just gone by was by chance sucked in just then under the boat's stern. The big propellers tore into the floating mass. And up rose a cloud of bright green flies. Rose up, fanned out over the boat, took rest, on every surface, deck, stanchions, bare arms, necks. And stung like needles.

They ran to cover.

"Menace to navigation," Tom yelled.

At midday the Capitaine invited the two of them to join him for lunch. The meal they had seen old N'goi preparing from their own stocks had seemed pretty plain, and they cheerfully left Reg and Josh to consume it between them. It proved to be a good move. The Capitaine did himself extraordinarily well.

There was an assiette of cold meats.

"This is elephant?" Tom asked, holding up a morsel of steak. "We're eating elephant?"

"But, of course, mademoiselle. I would not lie to you."

Then there was a magnificent fish, bought, the Capitaine said, from a fisherman whose pirogue had come alongside only an hour earlier.

"It is called the Capitaine fish, mademoiselle. The Capitaine. I am eating myself, yes? But, I tell you, this country of the Capitaine fish, she has eaten me. To my very bones."

"You like the life here then?"

"Like it, ma chère. I tell you, it is perfection. I have work that I can do as I please. Every day I have food such as you are eating now. This wine we are drinking comes from France, yes? It is expensive, true, but I do not have much else to pay for. And..."

He stroked the strands of long black hair at the back of his bald skull with unmistakable complacency.

"And as for women," he said, "here there are never any difficulties. Here they know what is enjoyment, and they take it."

"But aren't there come-backs?" David could not help asking. "Indigestion? Aids?"

The Capitaine rumbled into laughter.

"Ah, yes, m'sieu. Sometimes there are the sharp pains in the stomach.

And one day, perhaps, yes, there will be Aids. But the end must come to all of us some day, and why not live in happiness till that time comes? Why not live, as I do, like a sultan? Because, you know, here on my boat I am a sultan. What I want, I have. What I say is to be done, is done. Perhaps not at once, but eventually."

He belched, making only the slightest attempt to restrain himself.

"It was not like that when I was first here, however," he said. "Not at all."

"You came to Africa like me then, Capitaine," David said with a smile. "An innocent?"

The eyes in the big, gross face twinkled.

"An innocent? Yes, in a manner, you could say I was an innocent. I was a busy innocent. You know, I learnt my calling on the Rhine. I ended as first mate on a Rhine cargo vessel. I worked hard there. We were never behind time. The boat was always shipshape, stem to stern. The crew was disciplined. And then, when I thought I would try the life here, I believed it would be the same."

"And it wasn't?"

"Oh, but, yes, it was. For some months, it was. For a year perhaps I tried to do everything in the way I was accustomed to. Lazy black bastards, I said, I'll show you how a ship should be run."

He turned and gave Tom the full benefit of a hotly admiring gaze.

"Mademoiselle. If I had kept that up for one more month, I would not be talking to you now. I would be buried somewhere at the edge of the Forest."

"But you had a revelation? You opted for the African way?"

"Exactly, ma chère. Except that I was no Saint Paul, and nothing special happened on my road to Damascus. It was simply that one day when I had fallen into yet another great rage I thought suddenly: why am I doing this? What is it that I am gaining? And there and then I began to live a different life. This life. My sultan's life."

He gave his wide stomach, which had issued two or three long rumbles, a pat.

"Now," he went on, "if I want to get drunk, I get drunk. I order the boat to stop and I do it. When I wish to eat, I eat. I eat what I want to eat. When I want a woman I make it known at the first village we come to, and a woman comes. Perhaps more than one. The sultan lives."

It was a merry meal indeed.

And afterwards David, slightly mazy from the wine, leaning again on the boat's rail watching the river slide by, said in a dreamily contemplative manner: "It's a wonderful life the lecherous old sod has."

"La vie Africaine," Tom said. "Like Thomasina's villagers at play on the sandbank."

"And she sort of sorry not to get an invitation to the party"

"That's it"

He turned towards her suddenly.

"How about us going to the party?" he said. "There's no need for the card with the gilt round the edge. We could jump ship at the next place we come to, wait for a riverboat eventually to come past going downstream, go back to the big city and live the sort of life the Capitaine lives, or any of those people we met there. The out-and-out happiness jag."

"Good God, I do believe you're working round to yet another bloody proposal."

"No, no. No, there'd be no need to get married for that sort of life. No commitments to it, you see. Just being, and being happy."

Tom looked at him assessingly.

"Serious?"

He lifted his chin, provoked.

"Not totally unserious," he said.

"No, you wouldn't be. I do believe you'd do it, too. Take me with you and leave poor Reg somewhere in the middle of Africa, with Josh probably not quite realising we were no longer with them, and all B-J's precious equipment. And then heigh-ho for a life of - of what actually?"

"Well, I said: happiness."

"But what do we do when we're having happiness? We can't just dance about all day."

"Well, we do what we want. That's the point of it all. We lie in bed, or we stay up all night. We just let it happen. And we could do it, you know. We could get odd bits of work, enough to get by. Bit of currency wangling. Wouldn't be difficult."

"I do believe you're actually contemplating it. Damn it, you'd abandon the Steps *of a Jungle Gentlewoman* just like that."

"Okay, I know we're supposed to be committed to it, contract with old B-J, all the rest. But that isn't the most important thing in the world, is it? It's just another TV documentary."

Tom pursed her lips.

"Yeah, I know," she said, "it's not any great mission to save mankind or anything. It's not even a tenth of what Thomasina's expedition was, finding that plant she believed would cure typhoid. And certainly I don't feel any obligation to B-J. But..."

"Doesn't tempt you? Me spreading before you all the joys of the anchorless life? No obligations? No duties? Nothing that has to be done today, or tomorrow, or any time? Just like Thomasina's Africans playing away on their sandbank, not a care in the world."

"Sandbanks get submerged again sooner or later. End of play."

"Well, as the Capitaine said, we've all got to come to an end one day. So why not have fun, happiness even, while we can. I mean it, you know."

For some long moments Tom said nothing. Below them the water rippled by. A long clump of jacinthe d'eau swept past. She watched it till the superstructure of the boat hid it from view.

"Yes," she said at last, "and I'm serious too. I can't do it. I don't quite know why, but I can't. I can see the attraction all right. I can see a sort of other-Tom, someone just beside me, like me in every way, doing it. Leaving everything for the happiness of life. But this Tom? No."

Now David was silent. And at last he spoke.

"Did I realise all along you'd say that? Was I making my play because I knew deep-down it wasn't actually going to lead to anything? I don't know. Perhaps I was."

"And perhaps you weren't. I could see you doing it, with or without me. For God's sake, it's the story of your life. Flitting from flower to flower. The young academic nosing into Conrad or whatever. The would-be actor, playing Hamlet at - where was it? Gateshead? The aspirant novelist, with the never-finished manuscript. And sculpture. Didn't you tell me you'd once thought of a sculpture?"

"More than thought. Spent nearly a year of my life at it. And I wasn't so bad either."

"But not actually good enough to make a go of it. And then the going-to-be hailed TV director."

"Who ended up churning out educational documentaries. Say it. And you've forgotten the advertising whizz-kid. Or did I never get round to mentioning that? Six months as a copywriter. They loved me. I didn't love them."

"Well, you get the point at any rate. I can absolutely see you suddenly plunging off into the African sprawl. I dare say you will still, even before we've found Thomasina's diaries."

"And you won't join me? Not never? Not even if we plighted our troth? In a whole cathedral?"

"Oh, I might. I might. And there wouldn't be any need for any plighting, as you said. But I won't do it while this job's still there. Not till the last reel's in the can. Editing done back in London. Commentary spoken. Every last bit. I'm sorry, Teigh, but that's the way I find I am. I'm surprised at myself really. But there it is. I can't see myself abandoning the plan, even if it is a fairly ridiculous plan we've conned B-J into backing. I just want to stick to it."

"The lady who revels in confusion," David said, with more sadness than hostility. "Who likes nothing better than everything going wrong."

"Well, that's fair, I suppose. But, surprise, surprise, I turn out also to want everything to go right. According to plan. Not exactly consistent. But who is?"

"Well you might say that Thomasina was but do you remember the time that she too had to accept that there was '*confusion in the Forest*'.

There have been scarcely four miles to be added to my tally for all this day's work. The trouble was a perfect beast of a stream. It was not tremendously wide, but deep it was and fierce, much grown in its sense of its own importance. As soon as we got near it Snail-Shell shouted to me above the horrid noise the thing was making that this was 'mauvais-mauvais'. A piece of information I could very well make out for myself. Even M'bene was cowed by the sight and made no attempt, in his usual manner with watery obstacles, to dash in and try his luck. "Si nous tombons," he said, peering at the hither-and-thither rush of the thing. "Tombez pas," I replied. I could think of no other solution. For an hour or more we searched upstream in hope of finding somewhere less fearfully turbulent. Then for a second hour we searched downstream. At last M'bene and Snail-Shell ventured in together at a spot where it looked as though there was a ridge of firm ground running crossways against the current – making a shocking boiling fuss all of its own. My heart was in my mouth as they struggled against the turmoil. More than once they both disappeared, though I told myself it was only under a fan of spray. Thankfully I was right because at last they emerged and clambered out on the far side. There M'bene cut a stout creeper and threw it over to us. Or, rather, threw it towards us, since the torrent defeated his best efforts. But, tossed up and down in the spate, there it was, a lifeline. I bethought me, by way of comforting myself, of all the various feats of strength my untalkative, ever-smiling Fito had performed since the start of our days in the Forest. Then, linking my arms firmly around his waist – mercifully they reached – I committed myself and him, poor fellow to the waters. We survived. There were, true, more than a few moments when battered, bewildered and as I have since discovered, bruised, I thought my whole quest was to end as a piece of flotsam in a long skirt swirled helplessly down an African stream. Well, truth to tell, in the wildness of it all I had no such grand, dramatic thought. There was only a dash of disappointment amid the welter and confusion in my head. However, at last Fito, the good fellow, found the end of the creeper M'bene had thrown and by its aid was enabled to drag his useless burden to safety. The uselessness I admit cheerfully. And, after it all, we were really none the worse for the nasty time we had had. Indeed, we were rather the better, if cleanliness is a quality to rank above others. A necessary hour or more of rest while I combed, with what thoroughness I could, my tangled hair, and we were able to make a little more progress before darkness threatened.

It turned out that neither Tom nor David had taken the Capitaine's description of his life-style sufficiently seriously. If I want to get drunk, he said, I get drunk, I order the boat to stop and I do it. Towards the evening of the second day, it appeared he wanted to get drunk. They had been proceeding steadily upriver. The Capitaine had been in the wheelhouse calmly directing the steersman to this side or that of island or sandbank according to the large chart in front of him, frequently amended as the river's whim shifted silt this way or that. Then there had come from him a sudden immense whoop.

They had looked up at the wheelhouse to see a wide grin all across his big jowly face. He was pointing to a village on the bank, no different as far as they could see from a score of others they had glided past. But at once the boat began manoeuvring towards it. They dropped anchor, and within minutes a whole fleet of pirogues, their oarsmen standing splendidly upright in them came out from the bank.

The Capitaine emerged from the wheelhouse.

"This place," he shouted, "I had forgotten. The palm-wine they make, it is the best on the whole river. And the women, too, they are not to be despised."

Evidently the villagers were well aware of the reason the boat had come to a halt. Each of the pirogues, they saw, carried a large palm-wine calabash. In most of them, too, there were seated young women, happily grinning, full forms wrapped in colourful bubus. Soon they were calling out across the sound-enhancing water with strident blossoming immodesty.

Caught between disappointment at the curtailment of the day's tally of miles and bubbling pleasure at the lively scene below – frankly voyeuristic in David's case – they watched the pirogues draw alongside and negotiations between crew and villagers begin. Within a few minutes calabashes were being hauled on board and various items of barter were being lowered.

"Look," Tom said, a smile of wonder on her face. "Do you see what's in that little bundle going down there? Fish-hooks. Just like the ones Thomasina carried as trade-goods. Things do go on, you know. Year after year after year. It adds up to something, a sort of permanence."

"Well, yeah. But look at what's in that little net the fellow there's beginning to lower now. Transistor dry cells. What price permanence there?"

The bartering went on. Shouts. Exchanges. Jokes. Cheerful insults. And finally various rope-ladders were sent banging and clattering down the boat's side and from the pirogues a whole boarding-crew of deliciously buxom, giggling creatures ascended, assisted from below by jolly hoisting of buttocks. Two of the girls had no sooner reached the deck than they linked arms and darting glances from huge eyes this way and that, made their way to the Capitaine's cabin.

"Two," David moaned.

"Don't go getting ideas."

"Ideas I've got. It's whether I'm going to put them into practice that's the question. Are you sure you meant what you said about that girl in the dance hall?"

"Up to you."

"It would only be a frolic. Frolic a deux, you might call it."

"I know. But let me remind you, mate. Our friend the Capitaine is about to embark on a gamble. A double gamble, actually. Chances are that at this very moment two lots of squirmy little Aids viruses are wriggling with delight at the prospect of homing in on a new target. Want to go for it yourself?"

David sighed.

"And if I did..."

Tom held up a traffic policeman's warning hand.

"So it's cleave," David said. "Cleave or fuck off, those your terms?"

From behind them, out of the Capitaine's cabin, came a series of delighted squeals.

"Oh God," David said, "Why is the world so unfair?"

CHAPTER 7

The Capitaine, who had been brisk as a button the morning after his palm-wine and two-woman debauch, announced that evening that they would not be able to move on all the following day. They had come to a slow halt at a place called Mbandaka, creeping into its port past enormous towering trees leaning over the placid tea-brown river. A huge church, seemingly part of another, altogether different landscape, some quiet Catholic town in France or Belgium, had appeared and been left astern. Now, the Capitaine said, he had had news of some cargo no one had known about. A whole day would be needed to load it.

Unexpectedly David fretted at the delay.

"For God's sake," he said to Tom, "company money is trickling away, you know, while we sit about. I've got to account to B-J, after all."

Tom grinned, the smile of pure pleasure lighting up in her solid face.

"You just tell him a lie," she said. "You tell him we began filming tomorrow, say. He'll know it's a lie. But he'll be happy. As long as it all looks okay on paper. In the paper world."

"Well, but actually..."

David drifted into confused silence.

"Actually...?" Tom teased.

"Oh, all right. I suppose it doesn't really matter. But there is still Major Yombton-Smith. He's waiting for us. He'll have made all sorts of arrangements."

"Oh, my poor Teigh, it's all getting to you. You actually got his name right."

That was enough to finally prick David's bubble of responsibility.

He gave a feeble grin.

"Okay, you win. I suppose. So, what'll we do? Sight-see? Don't think there's any point in filming."

"Absolutely none. So let's see what delights wherever-this-is has on offer."

"Mbandaka. That's what the Capitaine called it"

Tom looked at him, her eyes impish.

"I knew really. And he actually said, too, it used to be called Coquihatville. Coquihatville. Nice. Sounds somehow delightfully irresponsible. Yeah?"

"Yeah. Irresponsible. What we actually both want. I think."

"You're learning, mate. It's the art of travel, as not written by Thomasina's Mr Galton."

"Then lead on, Macfluff."

They wandered off, vaguely making their way towards the two tall towers of the huge church they had seen the evening before. It seemed to be the only point of destination in sight.

Plainly, the town had once been flourishing. They had passed enormous brick-built warehouses as they had set out, though their wide entrances were dark and deserted, their walls softly crumbling. Now they came to big, almost stately houses bordering the wide red laterite road, empty all but for a single tethered goat. The paint that had made their veranda columns bright had long ago peeled away. Their gardens, laid out once it was just possible to discern in neat beds, were now tangled in rioting vegetation.

Such shops as they had seen appeared, too, to have been either abandoned or to be offering only the scantiest of stocks. No one, under the fiercely strong sun, had seemed much interested in disposing of such goods as they had.

From time to time as they strolled on there were glimpses between the big decaying mansions of the river, its distant bank only intermittently visible through the heat haze. Various abandoned vessels, a dredger, a launch, lay just out into the stream. Into one, a small stern-wheel paddle steamer, lianas from a tree over-hanging the water had swooped down and made their way, wriggling like so many serpents, through broken windows and across the dilapidated deck. It was as though Africa was proliferatingly determined to take this mechanical intrusion into its many-tongued maw and digest it out of existence.

"Not very cocky, Coquihatville, after all," Tom said. "But, actually, I rather like it all the same. I could just – just – see myself spending the rest of my life here. Floating."

"What I wanted you to do in the city, but here instead?" David asked, darting in. "Bit different, of course, but essentially much the same."

He gave her a quick, inquiring glance.

"Beginning now?"

Tom laughed.

"Beginning after Steps *of* is wrapped up," she said. "And probably not then. But it has got something, this place."

"Oh, yes. It may be a dump in many ways. Look at the port area. But, yes, it's got charm. Or no, more than charm. Allurement. How about that? I think it must be the lushness of everything. Those trees. So tall, and growing, growing. That bush there – would it be bougainvillaea? – quietly sprawling away, taking over. It's entropy time, you know."

"Entropy?"

"Sorry. Smart word. Meaning, as far as I remember, the tendency of everything to decay leading in the end to formless chaos. Has its attractions."

"Perhaps," Tom said.

"Well, I reckon it's that that's making you want to spend the rest of your life here."

"You do? I think it's just Africa. You know we're almost bang in the bloody middle of it now. On the equator. Capitaine told me."

"Yeah. But I still favour entropy. Formlessness. Lost in it. Perhaps one day we really will find ourselves entropying here. Mooning. Mooning from dawn till dusk. Mooning and fading. Fading into the sprawl of it all."

"Hmm?"

It was impossible to tell whether the vague questioning sound indicated agreement or disagreement.

They strolled on. In silence.

Then, softly at first but soon becoming louder as they moved slowly through the heavy-scented air, there came the sound of drumming.

"It's drums," David said.

"Well, what did you think it was? The patter of tiny feet?"

"No. No, but I mean, drums. Native drums. Tom-toms. Sinister. Well, a bit. And now, anyhow, what's with you and the tiny feet? You're not - good Christ, you're not beginning to think deep-down about the other alternative, about starting a family?"

"You were the one who was all for marriage not so long ago."

"Well, yes, I was. Before. But I seem to have gone off the boil a bit now. Don't know why. Probably the atmosphere here. Or monsieur le Capitaine and his sultan life."

"And sultans never marry?"

"Well, only by the dozen, and that's different. But, Christ, listen to those drums. I mean - well, you can understand, can't you?"

"Understand what?"

"All the books, the legends. All the white man's grave stuff and missionaries in the pot. I mean, when you hear that sound."

"Well," Tom said, coming to a halt, "I don't think we're in actual danger of succumbing to one of those jokes at this moment."

"May be not."

David stood listening to the insistent throbbing filling the silence of the sleepy town.

"But we're only at the edge here," he said. "There's all the Forest to come. And God knows what could happen there."

"You'll get bitten by some rather nasty insects, I expect. And I won't"

David gave her a glare.

The drums beat on. Ceaselessly, rhythmically.

"You don't think," he said, "that we ought to sort of wander back? I mean, it seems to be coming from near the church somewhere."

"No, I do not think we should turn tail. If we're going to make a daring film about discovering Thomasina's diaries in the middle of the rainforest, you've got to learn to be a big brave boy."

"Well, yes. I know, I know. But I do have to protect the little woman, too."

The drumming was loud now, totally a part of the quivering air rising up from the flat red road ahead.

"You remember that big Zairean guy we met who was either an expert on ancient Africa or a con artist?" David asked.

"Yup. Very hot on – what did he say? – the world of the night. The time when, according to him, Africans have everything that Europe has, only it all vanishes away with daylight?"

"That's him. Well, he said, too, that drums like these imitate human voices. That's the way messages get sent incredible distances, fast as the speed of sound."

"I believed that anyhow," Tom said. "Didn't you?"

"Oh, yes. I even wondered if we could use it in the film, to illustrate Thomasina. Only I thought it'd be too complicated. But, well, what do you think these drums are saying now?"

Tom grinned.

"Probably two nice whites coming up," she said. "Suitable for boiling, roasting or deep-frying."

"Oh, don't be silly. Listen."

They stood paying full attention to the insistent throbbing rhythms.

"If you ask me," David said, with a shake of his head, "I'd actually have to give it as my opinion that the message they're sending is something like *Hymn tunes for all, cut price till Saturday.*"

"Clever boy. Because that's just what they are saying. You know where they're actually coming from?"

Tom was smiling all over her face.

"Inside the church?" David said. "Oh, no, I refuse to believe it."

"Seeing's believing. Let's look."

Tom led the way rapidly up the incline to the rearing bulk of the church. And, as soon as they reached the huge brick-built edifice, they could see through the open doors a scattering of worshippers and, incongruous in white surplices up near the distant altar, a group of Africans quietly singing to the accompaniment of two drummers, broad backs bent over their wide instruments.

"Creep in?" Tom asked.

David took a pace forward, then stopped.

"No," he said. "No. Don't think so."

"Singing's super. Marvellous deep voices."

"Yes, I know. But it's creepy, too, rather, isn't it? Not creepy like Tom-Toms, because it's somehow all wrong."

He turned resolutely away. Tom went with him.

"I'm sorry," he said after a little. "But I just hated the thought of it all. I don't know. It seemed like a terrible, futile, pathetic attempt to impose order on - on what isn't ordered. Those drums beating out that rhythm, not to send any message, but to try to say everything's right, everything's good. God's in his heaven and we're thumping out some nice music."

"Know what you mean," Tom said. "Though, of course, you're making too much of a fuss about it. But that's you."

"Thank you. But do you really know what I mean?"

"Oh, yes. It's sort of pasting a cosmetic layer over the whole seething turbulence of Africa. What no one quite wants to speak about."

"Yes. Yes, it's regularity pretending to be order. And order's more than just regularity. Don't exactly know what it is, but it has to be more than that, whether one wants it or not."

"Okay. But don't take it so much to heart. Don't let Africa get to you. Not when we haven't even penetrated into the primeval jungle."

"That's my line," David pounced.

He grinned, a little pallidly.

"Anyway," he said, "I'd like to get away from the sound of those drums. Won't there be somewhere we can get a drink?"

It did not take them long, walking back a slightly different way, to come across an ancient hotel showing some signs of life. They entered, saw a painted sign saying *Bar merican*, and made their way into it.

It was deserted, all but for a solitary barman in a much-pleated magenta shirt. He was standing behind the brass-rimmed bar – one whole strip of the brass was curling upwards as if it had taken on vegetable life – and had apparently simply not noticed their arrival.

The whole long room, under its low ceiling from which hung a row of wide-bladed fans conspicuously failing to circulate the torpid air, had a feeling of existing in forgotten time. The plastic-faced clock above the bar had stopped at twenty to five. For sale underneath it there were no more than eight or nine bottles, ranged at intervals on dusty shelves. It was just possible in the shadowy gloom to make out that there was one of Ouzo, two Lamb's navy rum, three with labels blotted out from damp, one of Crème de Cacao and some brands of whisky with names unknown to man.

The barman continued to ignore them even when they had come right up to the bar. He moved from one bottle to another, minutely adjusting their positions.

"Bonjour, citoyen," David said loudly

His voice sounded alien as if it came from the sound-track of a film other than the one they were in.

"Deux whisky, s'il vous plait."

The barman turned to face them, but made no reply. Instead he thrust two fingers into the pocket of his luminous shirt, extracted a packet of cigarettes and lit one, tremblingly.

"Deux whisky," David repeated.

Now the barman, still without a word, turned back to his bottles, spent a few moments looking from one anonymous whisky bottle to another, eventually selected one, seemingly at random, and poured two drinks.

They retreated to the far end of the room. The barman resumed his self-imposed task of adjusting the positions of the bottles. In one corner a big white fridge abruptly juddered into life.

"You know," David said, "what I'd actually like to do is to visit one of those witchcraft merchants we heard about from our ethnicity friend. See the real religion of Africa instead of that awful superimposed hopelessness. You remember what our friend said about them?"

"Yeah. That's all very well. But you know what we'll be confronted with. Entrails of cockerels, disembowelled spiders big as saucers, disgusting smells."

"No, it'd be interesting. Really. A closer look at the Africa that you feel all around you and that's tantalisingly just out of sight."

"But do you really want to see it? Can't we just sail through it, round it, over it? With civilisation clasped to us, like the sheet when someone comes banging into the bedroom?"

"Now who's not being brave?"

Tom grinned, her eyes glinting with mischief in the gloom.

"You certainly know how to bend a girl to your will," she said.

"Ought to. Been practising on you for three solid years, haven't I?"

"You have. You have. You know, we are used to each other, no getting round that. Do you think -"

She broke off.

"Take a gander over there," she said.

In the doorway, faintly lighter from the harsh sunlight out-side, there stood a familiar figure. Old N'goi.

He came up to them.

"Vous voulez visiter un féticheur?"

They looked at each other.

"Yes, but how -" David began. "I mean, comment est-ce que vous saviez çela?"

"Je le savais," old N'goi replied.

David turned to Tom.

"Best answer we'll get, I suppose," he said. "But all the same it's bloody mysterious."

Tom sighed.

"He was probably lurking just outside and heard us talking"

"But we were speaking English."

"And how do you know he doesn't understand English? At least some?"

"Oh, all right. Have your logical explanation, if you must. But secretly I'm going to believe it's magic. African magic."

He turned to N'goi.

"Lead, kindly light," he said.

"Pardon, m'sieu?"

David shot Tom a glance.

"Could be a bluff," she said.

"Okay, okay. And mon ami, oui, nous voulons visiter un whatsit - féticheur. On peut y aller tout de suite?"

N'goi turned and beckoned them to follow.

He led them down a lane beside the hotel. There were thorn hedges to either side and occasionally a tumbledown ochre-coloured hut. From one a dog rose lazily to its feet and offered an uninterested bark. They turned one corner, then another. The path dwindled into a mere wandering track. Red dust covered their shoes.

At last they came to a small hamlet or settlement, apparently on the very outskirts of the town. Beyond there was forest. It was not the dense jungle of the banks of the river, all immense trees and thickly interlaced lianas. Instead it was a scrubby growth of saplings and bushes interspersed with tall clumps of grasses. The concrete huts of the place were set in a close huddle with only narrow bands of softly powdery red earth between them. They appeared to have been built without any plan, so that the fronts of some faced near the rear of others. In open cooking-sheds fires glowed sullenly between blackened stones. Women could be seen tending them, stirring languidly at round aluminium cooking-pots or nursing babies. Children crawled to and fro, dirty and dribbling.

N'goi stopped in front of a hut looking no different from any of the others. He called out a name they failed to catch.

In a moment a man came to the hut's door. He was not a prepossessing figure. The baggy orangey robe he wore over bony shoulders was grease-splashed and torn at the foot. Nor did two heavy necklaces of large brown beads do anything to add dignity to his appearance. On his head, at an angle, was an ancient black trilby hat, battered and greening.

N'goi addressed him in some native language. A long desultory conversation followed. At last N'goi turned to them.

"You must give him two thousand," he said in his clear French.

David glanced over to Tom.

"Too much?"

"Probably. But it's not actually a vast sum, is it? So go ahead, if you must."

David fished out the necessary notes and handed them to the féticheur, if féticheur he was.

When he turned back to Tom he found that old N'goi had vanished.

"Where's he gone?" he barked. "How the hell do we get back to civilisation?"

"The way we came," Tom said equably. "Though whether what we reach is civilisation is another matter."

"Yes. Well... well, I suppose we're in for it now."

The féticheur was urging them inside.

The room he led them into was drearily depressing. Its furniture consisted of an iron bedstead without a mattress, a wicker armchair broken in several places and a wicker stool. On the acid-green walls, which were patched here and there with darker grime where people had leant, there hung two crudely-printed calendars. One was years out of date, and the other was for the right year but the wrong month. An umbrella was hooked over a large nail with three or four objects made out of feathers beside it. They might have been masks or they might have been almost anything else. There was a strong smell of urine.

On the bedstead lay a head-dress of tall feathers. The féticheur picked it up, took off his hat and put it on.

"Now I will cut my hand and in one minute it will be healed,"

He muttered in French it was only just possible to follow.

"Are you going to let him?" Tom asked David.

"Well, I suppose he knows what he's doing. And we have paid him all that money."

The féticheur left the room and returned after a few moments with a long knife in his right hand and his left hand carefully clenched.

He turned to face the darkest corner of the room, lit only by a narrow barred window opening. He raised the knife dramatically high. And plunged. At once he turned back to them, flashed his left palm open for just long enough to show a red line that might have been a cut. Then he hugged it close again.

"Oh, God," Tom said. "It's not even a well-done trick."

"I'm sorry," David answered. "I don't know, I suppose when old N'goi appeared in that mysterious way I thought he'd be bound to take us to see the real thing."

The féticheur came up and thrust out his hand, clearly uninjured though slightly red-smeared.

"Oh, go away," David said.

There was a confused noise, shouting and loud voices, outside. Then, without ceremony, a number of people came bursting into the room. They were carrying the body of a young woman.

She would have been about twenty and had been wearing a red bubu whose end trailed on the ground. She hung, a limp bundle, from the arms of the two men holding her. Her eyes were wide open showing their whites.

"Oh, God," David said. "A corpse. Why does this have to happen to us?"

"You're sure she is a corpse?" Tom asked. "I mean, do you think she's been killed, or just died? Or what?"

"I - I don't know. I suppose I could try and get a closer look and make sure."

Reluctantly David approached the bedstead on which the woman's body had been lowered, somewhat cursorily. No one seemed inclined to prevent him peering down at her.

She showed no signs of being alive. The skin of her face and lips was of so dull a grey that it was hard to believe blood could be flowing underneath.

Cautiously he took a wrist and searched for a pulse. For a minute, for two, he moved his fingers across the firm flesh. But he could find no trace of a heartbeat.

He looked across to Tom.

"Dead," he said. "Dead, I'm sure. Well, almost. Must have been some sort of seizure. I - think we could safely sort of steal away."

"Okay."

But before they could work their way through the crowd of onlookers – more were squeezing in at every moment – the féticheur began giving orders in a loud, confident, hectoring voice.

Through the doorway what looked like a bundle of straw was handed in and passed rapidly over the heads of the crowd till it reached the bedstead. There eager helpers unfolded it and wrapped it round the body of the girl. It seemed to be a dress or petticoat made of long lengths of grasses bound together. Various pots of liquids began to arrive, and from them the girl's face, arms and hands were daubed in thick red and yellow.

Then the féticheur lifted up his head and began a loud harsh crooning. From somewhere just outside someone started beating a drum. Its rhythms assaulted the ears, as insistent but more urgent than the sound they had heard coming from the big church.

All round, the thickly crowded onlookers began to shuffle back and forth in a kind of rhythmic dance.

David looked at Tom. There was hardly any hope of getting out of the jam-packed room. Tom shrugged. Bit by bit they managed at least to work their way closer to each other up against one of the walls. The drumming grew louder, more urgent. The féticheur's voice rose to a high wailing. The dancing increased in pace and vigour. The smell of sweat, of breath, of body-oil, of crude perfumes, became almost overpowering.

And there on the bedstead – they both saw it clearly – the body of the girl twitched.

It took about five minutes more of thudding dancing, insistent drumming and the féticheur's harsh wailing before she sat up. Then, almost at once, she slid off the bed and began, thickly shuffling at first but soon with full energy, to dance along with the rest of the jam-packed onlookers.

David and Tom exchanged glances.

"I don't believe it," David said. "I refuse to believe this has happened."

***

Old Snail-Shell had halted at intervals all the afternoon to listen to the sound of distant drumming. To Thomasina it had been hard to

78

hear, coming to them as it was muffled by the deep canopy of leaves high above, branch after branch interlayered and interlaced. But to Snail-Shell it had been clear enough. The drums were saying, he had told her, that there would be a storm that night. A mighty storm.

She had little difficulty in believing him. His readings of drum messages on other occasions had given her considerable respect for his abilities.

Now, as he had promised, the storm, witnessed much earlier many miles away and reported in drumming more swiftly than any bird could fly or man run, had arrived. And it was mighty indeed. High, high above, the force of the wind sent the great trees threshing and struggling in the darkness.

Thomasina could feel the vibrations from it right at the base of the huge mahogany under which they were sheltering, apparently as unshakable as Salisbury cathedral itself. But it's ancient wood, ring upon ring through the ages, was positively humming.

Were the others awake, she wondered. Should she rouse herself and add some wood to their fire? But, no, its glow seemed steady. It should defy all but the heaviest drenching when the rain started to fall. And, so far, the others, ritualistic old Snail-Shell, impetuous M'bene and young, silent, just smiling Fito, seemed not to have been disturbed by the noise and thrashing of the wind above.

Soon the rain began. At first it came as only a few drops, heavy as egg-cupsful of water, splashing on to the leaf layer above. Then weighty dollops began to splash on to the oozy ground all round. And, before long, they were in the midst of a battering rain-pour.

Snail-Shell was the first to be woken by it. He sat up and at once began to go through some ceremony designed to ward off this particular evil, scooping water from the ground beside him and with much muttering, swallowing it from his cupped hands. Within a minute or two M'bene and Fito had also left their branch beds. By the dull light of the fire, Thomasina thought that Fito at least was looking far from happy. Certainly the storm seemed to be as bad or worse than any she herself had encountered in her days and nights in the Forest.

But the enormous mahogany at her back was marvellously reassuring.

Yet the wind was increasing in mad turbulence at every instant. The tree behind her had ceased humming and was giving out deep groans and creaks. Worthy, she thought, of any ghost in a fireside winter story.

She made up her mind not to be frightened by the noises, any more than she had ever been, other than deliciously, by the tales of spook and hobgoblin. In any case, being scared, however thoroughly, could be of no possible help.

Nor did she feel inclined to pray. It had been a long while, in truth, since she had said any prayers. Somehow within the Forest depths it seemed as if the eye of God did not penetrate. Or else she was in a wholly different world. A world over which a deity had no jurisdiction, not even Père Jossuet's jealous God.

But now the great mahogany was actually moving, swaying massively from side to side right down to its vast base behind her. The rain was lashing down, too, its drops as heavy as ever but descending now with force of stones from a sling.

Should she pray after all?

Behind her, as if in answer to her question in the depths of her mind, the mahogany gave an even mightier groan. She seemed to feel the ground beneath the mat of branches she had been sleeping on actually heave.

And at once it happened.

The great tree lurched to the side. The ground beneath its roots, shallow and spreading for all the tree's enormous height, reared upwards.

Thomasina was tumbled headlong from her couch of branches. She saw that she was rolling towards the hissing glow of the fire. With a desperate swing of her body she managed to keep to the side. She was aware all around her of shrieking pandemonium. A roaring, sweeping movement. Dark chaos. Fito screaming with the full might of his lungs. Brands from the fire hurtling through the rain-swamped air.

And the tree – immense, cathedral-safe – was swishing downwards.

The huge tearing screech as its great branches dragged through the branches of its brother trees all round deafened all thinking. The earth, as the roots were tugged from it, gave a vast hollow sucking shriek.

Above her, as she turned to look upwards, she saw a huge branch swinging out of the darkness on to her. She shut her eyes, dimly expecting her last moment.

But that moment did not come. Something altered the course of the descending branch, caught it and halted it some feet above her. Then there came a final earth-trembling jar as the mahogany's massive trunk finally struck the ground.

And, not silence, because the wind was tearing still at the leaf canopy high above and the rain was beating like stones on the earth all around, not silence, but with the ending of the noise of that great fall, a comparative quietness.

Thomasina lay where she was. Above her she could make out, against the lighter look of what was overhead, the leaves, twigs and lesser branches of the huge limb that had so nearly come down on her. Her mouth, she found, was full of cut and torn fragments of leaf. The rain was beating on to her body sharply as if her sodden dress was no longer there.

She spat the debris out and called into the darkness.

"Are you safe? Where are you?"

Two voices replied at once, M'bene's and Snail-Shell's. Then, a heart-wrenching moment afterwards, there came Fito's.

She lay quietly where she was.

Was this the time to pray? To offer thanksgiving? But nothing in her mind seemed to tell her that it was.

At last the rain began to slacken. Then it ceased. With caution, she tried getting to her feet. Her head became entangled in the lower part of the huge branch almost on top of her. She pushed clear, ducking and wrenching and eventually found a place where she could stand upright.

A pallid light was falling into the wide wasteland created by the mahogany's battering descent. Moonlight.

She looked up. The last ragged clouds of the storm were scudding away. A star-pointed sky was revealed.

Stars, she thought, I have not seen a single star for weeks, creeping along as I have been beneath that great leaf-heaven stretching and stretching unbroken before and behind.

Then, majestically, a wide moon beam began to steal across the new-made, tangled, chaotic clearing. It caught the white of the torn wood. It showed earth-clung roots left high in the air above. The last threshings of the branches of the trees surrounding the devastated area died away. A huge tranquillity spread over everything.

M'bene came up and asked, in a voice unusually hushed, if she knew where her Lucifer matches were.

She looked round and saw, not five feet away, her leather bag which till the cataclysm had come she had been using as a pillow. She picked it up, opened it and found its contents in a hopelessly confused jumble. But after a moment she was able to spot the soap-box, in which she always kept the matches for dryness' sake, and extracted one for M'bene. A single Lucifer was always enough for any one of them to get a fire going.

She set down the bag and stood looking up again at the sky. Before long she found herself slipping into a trance of quietness. It was, she thought dreamily, not the wild beauty of the moonlit scene that was holding her, though a wild beauty it did have. It was, more, a gradually encroaching feeling of being at one with everything that surrounded her. At one with the Forest.

Minutes seemed to pass. She was hardly aware of it when the others coaxed a new fire into life, though she vaguely realised it was there, a bright blaze. She was aware, too, just as dreamily, that the three of them had settled themselves round it, dark huddled shapes. But she stayed where she stood, unmoving. She was soaked through and through, and even knew that she was shivering and ought to seek the fire's heat. But she felt no inclination to do so.

She seemed so much to be a part of the whole serene, storm-past Forest, quietly breathing above and around her that she could only stay and bathe in the tranquillity that had, miraculously entered into her, swept through her, in the wake of the appalling sound and fury of the typhoon. Somehow, she thought, or perhaps felt only, it had been a baptism for her. Her baptism into the creed of the multifarious Forest.

CHAPTER 8

Halted at yet another indistinguishable village to take on board a waiting stack of timber, the Steps *of a Jungle Gentlewoman* party leant against the rail of the boat and watched the loading process. It was at best spasmodic. The Capitaine showed little interest and both the crew and the villagers were going about the task in a mood of aimless, happy lethargy.

Reg Blandy was extremely disapproving.

"Not how I was brought up to go about things," he said, a condemnation he had already voiced half a dozen times. "We wouldn't have lasted long, would we, Josh, if we'd worked like that when we had our way to make."

"Um?"

"For goodness sake, don't you ever listen to what's said to you?"

"Oh, sorry. No. No, I was thinking."

"And no good asking what you were thinking about. I've learnt my lesson there. Were you even looking at those layabouts dickering with those planks?"

"Planks? Oh. Oh, yes, I was looking. Really."

"Well, it's a scandal, isn't it? I mean, it's other people they're holding up. I don't suppose they even think of that. And we've got a job to do, if nobody else has."

"That's my Reg," David was unable to stop himself butting in. "Can't wait to get down to pointing the lens at every inch of the primeval jungle."

"No, Reg is right," Tom said unexpectedly. "We are here to make a film, and till we get into the Forest there's nothing more to be done. And I wish you'd stop calling it primeval jungle."

"Well, that's what it is, isn't it? And, you know, I've a notion that when we do plunge into its depths you may find it rather more than you've bargained for, Theresa Olivia Mountjoy. Come to that I dare say I will, too"

Tom looked at him, with a hint of suspicion, brought up short by his use of her mouthful of a full name.

"Okay," she said, "I may never have been in the rainforest, but I don't see that it'll be all that different from other off-the-map places I've worked in. Not fundamentally."

"No?"

"No," she said with a tiny burst of indignation. "Anywhere remote, it's just a matter of not knowing exactly what's going to happen from one day to the next. One hour to the next, even. And that's what I happen to like."

David smiled at her.

"Well, you may be right," he said. "Though, I must admit, I do have this notion that the primeval jungle is out on its own somehow."

"Oh, damn that. You're not coming over all old N'goi again, are you?"

"Okay. But all the same old N'goi is - I don't know. A small advance warning?"

Reg popped himself back into a conversation that had been taken away from him.

"I must say he's not a person I take to, your Mr N'goi. I'd call him creepy really."

"So long as he keeps on cooking as well as he creeps," Tom said. "It makes a hell of a difference, decent food. I learnt that the first time out, in Afghanistan."

"Listen," David said, "I'll make a bargain with you. You never mention Afghanistan again and those birds you and your school chum filmed, and I'll lay off the primeval jungle. Okay?"

But over on the river bank the business of getting the timber on to pirogues to bring out to the boat had taken a new turn. From a hut at the far side of the village a curious figure had emerged. He was a man in late middle age who appeared to be dressed in altogether unusual splendour. A wide yellow-green robe hung from his shoulders to his

85

feet and an enormous shiny crucifix, quite large enough to be made out in the bright sun from the boat's deck, dangled from his neck.

As he came to the water's edge it was apparent he was also wearing a pair of sunglasses with one lens missing. Tucked under his arm he had a red-backed plastic clipboard.

His arrival at once caused a stir among the lethargic workers at the timber stack. They became at once noticeably more earnest. The reason was soon apparent. As each new plank was laid across the pair of pirogues ferrying the timber out to the boat the man in the wide yellow-green robe was recording it with a tick on his red clipboard. Order had entered in.

Or so it appeared.

Because, after the work had been going steadily on for perhaps half an hour more, and one pirogue-load had been brought out, David, who had taken to watching the scene through binoculars, suddenly gave a hoot of laughter.

"Hey," he said, "you know what that fellow's using to tick off each loaded plank?"

"Using?" Tom said. "A pencil or something. A ballpoint? How should I know?"

"But he's not. He's using a stick. A thick twig that can't be making any more of a mark than if it's an india-rubber."

"You're quite right," Reg Blandy put in, peering hard at the scene on the bank. "I like to think I see more detail than most. I mean, I've got a trained eye. But you had me there, Dave."

"I'll tell you something else then. I ought to have cottoned on to it from the first: he's a madman, our friend in the yellow frock. A loony."

"Of course," Tom said. "Of course. I should have realised, too. I saw enough madmen wandering about on the loose when I was in Kenya for the Kilimanjaro film. I suppose it's just the same here."

"It shouldn't be allowed, if you ask me," said Reg. "there ought to be places for people like that."

"Oh, I don't know," David countered. "Madmen don't do any harm, most of them. It's only that they're disturbing. Glimpses of the borderline. That way chaos lies. For all of us."

A hint of a grin crossed his face.

"You should know that, Reg," he said. "After all, you and that chappie over there have got a lot in common. Passion for checking everything off."

Reg reddened in a pouter-pigeon rage.

"Are you saying that I'm not in my right mind?"

"No, no. Just that we're all of us nearer the edge than we pretend, that's all. Our friend with the thick twig is just on the other side of it from us. Only just. And actually, we've got something to thank him for. He's doubled the work rate there on the bank."

But Reg was not pacified. He stood, stiff and tense as if he had been abruptly turned to concrete.

Tom hastened to the rescue.

"Do you remember Thomasina's meeting with a madman?" she said into the air. "It was almost as soon as she'd arrived in Africa. While she was getting her canoe crew together. In Boma, I think."

I have been attempting to befriend a poor maniac. It is not something I ever thought I would find myself doing, and it is certainly not what I came to Africa to do. But the fellow, who was quite the blackest and tallest African I had yet seen, had chosen to inhabit the shore of the river just below my lodging, and the howlings he let forth in the watches of the night so disturbed me that I took it into my head that I might do something to make his life easier. It was a foolish thought, as I knew very well that none of the good people of the neighbourhood saw it as in any way their duty to succour the poor creature, though plainly from the energetic way he leapt and capered about the strand by day he was not going without sustenance. Maniacs are suffered to go at large here in a way that in England would never be countenanced. I am told that, if they show signs of being dangerous, trouble is taken to chain them to some convenient tree, a fate I am inclined to think rather more agreeable than a dark cell in a bedlam. However, in despite of local custom, I set out the day before yesterday to visit my poor man, taking with me as a token of goodwill a handful of sweet biscuits. My first overtures met with no success at all. My fellow at once took off helter-skelter as fast as his long legs would carry him.

Undeterred, I repeated the experiment as soon as I saw through my window (if that is the word for the barred aperture which in dear, chilly Salisbury would have been filled with glass panes) that he had come wandering back, apparently in a less nervous frame of mind. This time I had better luck. I saw that he had taken note of the biscuits in my hand and knew them for what they were. Yet he still did not dare approach, however delicately I extended my sugary bait. Eventually I set down the little feast on a clean rock, withdrew a short distance and watched. It took many a minute and much wild capering, but eventually the rock was reached and my offering consumed. Consumed in a flash, I may add. Then yesterday I was permitted to stand within a few feet of the rock while the bait was taken. I even ventured a smile, and was rewarded, I think, with something of the same nature in return. But now today I find the fellow gone. I have made enquiries, but no one is able, or perhaps willing, to tell me anything, bar a few conjectures of a somewhat grisly nature. However, unless he comes back as mysteriously as he had disappeared I shall have quiet nights henceforth, and I find the idea not unpleasing.

"You know," Tom said, "for someone like Thomasina, brought up in the Close at Salisbury, probably not seeing anything more alarming than a runaway horse from one year's end to the next, to go and try and make friends with a madman, let alone one who was black and big, was quite something."

"Oh, yes," David said. "You don't have to sell the lady to me."

"So what are we going to find in those diaries 'to be continued'?"

"If we ever get to that place they're supposed to be hidden."

"Oh God, you're not contemplating abandoning us again, are you?"

"No, no. Passing whim, that. Not that I might not have acted on my whim. Specially if you'd agreed to come. But, no, I think you're okay for a bit anyhow. No, it was more I was thinking we might not succeed in our jungle quest any more than Thomasina did in hers really."

"She just found her quest had a different object. Her Atembogunjo."

"All right, I suppose in those terms you could say she succeeded. In the arms of her chunk of Forest lover. But what I meant was that there's a hell of a lot of dodgy circumstances between us and those diaries."

"No, no. You're wrong. I didn't go into all this without weighing the odds, you know. And B-J certainly wouldn't put his pennies into anything that didn't stand a good chance of paying off."

"But think of all it depends on. Whether we can get hold of this Tim Lunn the prospector or not. Whether he'll play ball if we do, and that doesn't sound too certain. Whether Major Brown-Yombton - no. No, sorry. Yombton-Smith. Whether he's all he's cracked up to be about getting through the trackless Forest. Even whether we're capable of coping with the trackless Forest ourselves."

"Well, about that at least I don't have any doubts. For one thing, it isn't trackless. You've only to think of Thomasina's note books to know that. For a lot of the last part of it she was actually following tracks round about that deep-in-the-Forest village she got to."

"Well, okay but-"

"No. And there's another thing. You seem to forget that I'm actually not without experience of making my way through unknown territory. I have made eight major documentaries, you know, besides my Afghanistan bird-watching one."

"Afghanistan? Right. Primeval jungle, primeval jungle, primeval jungle."

Tom glowered.

"You know," she said, "there are moments when I think you're as far round the twist as our loony supervisor on the bank there. I tell you, I wish I had sane old Thomasina as my companion. She'd be a hell of a lot more reliable than you."

"Oh, would she?"

***

M'bene is dead. I fear it is through my fault. I believed until today that I had mastered the Forest. Poor fool that I am. Oh, my dear good friend of old, somehow in these past months I have ceased to address this diary to you, for whom though you would never see its pages, it was intended. I had begun to be proud. I saw myself as a conqueror sufficient to myself, however much a weak woman. I set down words here as a record of my triumphs. I had thought that I had triumphed over the Forest, despite the warnings of Mr Sparrhawk and, more threatening, those of Père Jossuet. But my triumphs are as dust. M'bene is dead, the man I had insisted on as leader of my little party, insisted on altogether against the judgement of kind Mr Sparrhawk, as I have now come to realise, because in that frank and happy smile of his and, more, even in the boastfulness, which I detected in him before I had known him for five minutes, I saw something that accorded with a strain in my own nature, a strain I felt had been suppressed in all the quiet years of my upbringing. But M'bene is dead, and I am to blame. Oh, Doctor, help me. Help me, though you cannot.

There had been a storm, not as fiercely devastating as the storm that had brought down the mahogany, but not to be ignored. It had come down on them as they had been struggling through a particularly densely growing area of Forest, and they had hastily gone back to an easier place to take shelter, a narrow gully they had passed about a quarter of an hour earlier. Then the little cleft had no more than a trickle of water at its foot as they had jumped across it. Now, already, a small swirling torrent two or three feet deep threatened to mount to a point where it would drag at their feet and legs as they clung to the bank. But the whole provided the best shelter they could hope for, and there they clung.

It was, as ever with a storm in the Forest, appallingly noisy. The rain was beating like a thousand dwarf drummers on the myriad leaves of the tree canopy high above. The wind was howling as it tossed the high branches wildly to and fro. Lianas, thick as a man's arm, smacked and cracked like devil's whips.

This is what it must be like, Thomasina thought, for a mouse cowering at the foot of wheat stalks in an autumn gale.

The notion brought back into her mind her childhood delight in the equinoctial gales. She recalled the trouble one of them had brought her once. It had been the sole occasion perhaps when her father, the mild canon, had punished her. She had been confined to her room on bread and water all the next long day. But woken by the rumbling boom of thunder and seeing even through the bed-curtains and the curtains across her window the dazzle of the lightning, she had slipped out of bed and gone to watch the sky-crossing display. Something in the wildness of it had drawn her to gasp at every jagged lighting-flash, to quiver in pleasure at each resounding thunder-peal.

And before long the rain had descended. It had beaten on the diamond panes of her window and streamed down them in sheets, and, beyond, distorting the shapes of the usually placid trees in their garden.

Then, on an impulse that even now thinking back to it she found unaccountable, she had seized the window handles, wrenched them upwards and flung open the twin casements. The rain had in an instant come swirling in. In two minutes her night-gown had become soaked. A glinting puddle had swiftly grown on the boards of the floor, lit in the repeated flashes of the lightning. But she had not cared. Somehow the flickering violence of it all had created in her a corresponding emotion. Never before in her quiet, ordered, obedient life had she felt any impulse like it. But there, then, she had thrust her head out of the window and stretched out to the storm as it had lashed at the neatness of the garden below.

Compared to the battering noise about her ears at this moment that storm had been no more than the puffings of a child with a straw wending paper-boats across a water-filled tub. But then it had been a heart-grabbing spectacle of magnificent unruliness. For half an hour, for longer, she had leaned out from her window. She had let the downpour beat on to her head and shoulders, oblivious of its chill. She had raised her face to the dark clouds and the gashing streaks of lightning. Each cracking boom of thunder had deafened and delighted her.

Only when the storm had moved away had she pulled off her soaked nightdress and crept, naked, back to bed. To be woken in the morning to maternal shock and paternal displeasure.

But, appallingly more dangerous though this equatorial onslaught was, it was also in its turmoil and violence entrancing.

Cautiously, to get a better sight of it, she began to raise her head above the level of the gully. She wriggled a foot on to a tough protruding root and hoisted herself some six or eight inches higher. To confront a sight utterly unexpected. And blankly terrifying.

Not six feet away from her unprotected face, lying flat to the ground, cowering before the might of the storm, was a leopard. Its forepaws were spread out in front of it as if it was attempting to grip the ground beneath for fear of being caught up and whirled away by the lashing this-way-and-that wind. The almond eyes in its blunt cat-face seemed to be staring straight at her. From its tensed jaw a deep, totally enraged growling was coming, loud enough to be heard even above the storm tumult.

She shrieked.

At once she wished, violently, that she had not done so. But she could no more have helped herself than she could have prevented herself falling had she been dropped from the basket of a flying hot-air balloon. The fear of the animal was so imprinted in her mind.

I would give anything, my dear dead friend beyond all helping me now in my distress, not to have let that scream of terror escape my lips. I truly believe I would give my life itself. But it had escaped my lips, or, indeed, my very soul. And it had reached the ears of my good, brave wretchedly impulsive M'bene. He looked up from where he was lying flat against the gully bank by my side. How could he not have looked up at that terrified cry? He saw what I was seeing. That beast crouched so near us, so filled with fierce feline rage. So ready, surely, to lash out in fear against any thing or creature it could vent its fury upon. Without an instant of hesitation my brave guide and companion loosened the machete from his belt, held it before himself like a pointing spear and plunged forward. Oh, he might have killed that beast. He could have done so. His was a wildly impulsive gesture, but not an entirely foolish one. But the beast was the quicker of the two. I saw it move, hardly seeing it amid the pandemonium of the rain and thunder. It was a blur. But a blur that was all intent to kill. And kill it did. It tumbled M'bene helplessly to the bottom of the gully, half in half out of the swelled stream rushing through it. It tore with rage at his throat. I had the courage then to seize my long waterproof bag from where M'bene had left it beside him, to stand tottering on the steep bank amidst the swirl of the rain and to hurl it with all the force I had in me. I threw well. The heavy weight of M'bene's burden, carried for so many Forest miles for me, struck the animal full on its back. In a moment it had leapt up the far side of the gully and had disappeared into the welter of the storm-struck Forest. But M'bene was dead. He was past all possible help. He was dead, and by my fault.

Although Thomasina had survived perhaps fifty Forest soakings – '*Rain-pours*,' she wrote in one of her memoranda books once, '*that left me thoroughly soppy and* miserable' – the wetting she received at the time of M'bene's death brought on next day a fever that rendered her incapable of travelling for a week and did not altogether leave her for a long time after that. She lay in the shelter Snail-Shell and Fito had built for her, the blood rioting in her veins, plagued in her mind by branding-irons of guilt.

When at last the fever began to abate and she was able to think with some approach to clarity about her situation she found she was incapable of deciding what she should do. One moment she would be certain that it was her duty to the memory of M'bene in his scratched grave at the side of the fatal gully to abandon Africa and make her way home, a penitent. Then the next, sometimes only minutes later, she would be equally convinced that she must complete the quest for which M'bene had laid down his life. She would think then that she owed it to him, that she owed it to Doctor Diver still, that she owed it even to the whole civilised world ravaged as it was from time to time by outbreaks of the deadly typhoid fever.

It was the latter thought that eventually took firmest root in her mind. There came a time when she felt strong enough to set out again. Solemn with grief, she re-arranged her three bearers' burdens so that they could be divided between old Snail-Shell and ever-willing Fito. She discarded as much as she could. The books she had on Doctor Diver's advice – yet had he truly meant her to venture into the Dark Continent? – brought with her to ward off Forest loneliness, Forest irrationality, Forest nightmares, she sacrificed first, Mr Darwin's *On the* Origin *of Species*, despite the giver, Mr Emerson's *Essays*, Boswell's account of Dr Samuel Johnson's fierce commonsense and terrible lapses into fear. Her revolver she disposed of, too. She took it when she was out of sight of the others and swiftly buried it, accepting in its place in her leather bag the remainder of her blank memoranda books. An instrument of death, however sensible it might be to have it in reserve, she could no longer bear to possess. A large portion of her trade goods she also left behind.

About her memoranda books she had debated for some time. But in the end she had kept them. She felt obscurely that they were a necessary lifeline. To a future when someone other than herself would read them? To a day in quiet Salisbury when, an old lady herself, she might muse upon the extraordinary expedition she had undertaken? She could not tell. But she could not make up her mind to abandon them.

Then she set out with her depleted party once more.

CHAPTER 9

"The horror, the horror," David murmured.

Tom turned to him, her solid face beneath the cap of springy hair showing mild surprise. Under their feet the boat chugged steadily on upriver.

"You all right?"

"Um? Oh, yes. I'm fine. I was just thinking."

"I see. And *the horror, the horror* is what happens inside there these days when you just think?"

"Oh, did I say it aloud? No, it's Conrad. I was having a bit of a muse about *Heart of Darkness* and what Mistah Kurtz must have actually come across in the Forest. Wondering really what sort of eye-openers there'll be there for us."

"You know I've never read the bloody book. Don't be so superior."

"Not being superior. It happens to be one of the masterpieces of English literature. Something everybody ought to have as part of the furniture. Or so I was taught at Cambridge."

"So you may have been. But that doesn't mean it's right. I don't have to have read it, if I never wanted to. That, or any other of your masterpieces."

It was David's turn to swing round in mild amazement.

"For God's sake, how can you say that? You're meant to be reasonably intelligent, reasonably aware of the way things are."

Tom drew herself up a little.

"That's exactly what I am," she said. "Aware of the way things are. And they're not the way it says in books."

"Oh, come on. That's what books - damn it, great literature, if you like, is there for. The books are guides, explorations, investigations. To tell us what it's all like."

"But they don't. That's just my point."

David looked at her, a hint of real anger showing on his broad face.

"For fuck's sake, how can you say that? I mean, it's all very well trying to be provocative, but this is simply an acknowledged fact. It's what novels, or at least the serious ones, actually do."

Tom tilted her chin at him.

"Well, they don't do it for me," she said. "They never did. Not when I was made to read them at school. Not whenever I've been pressured into trying them since."

"But - but you just can't mean that."

She smiled, a little de haut en bas.

"But I do. They're all the same, you know, your great masterpieces. All novels, come to that. They pretend to tidy things up. They try to make it all seem plain. And it isn't. And, what's more, I wouldn't like it if it was.

David shook his head in genuine bewilderment.

"But - you just don't understand. That's what they're written for, the best novels, the great novels. Well, all novels to some extent. To shake away the obscuring dross, to show us what it's all fundamentally like. Or at least what one bit of it at a time is like."

"And that's exactly why they get it wrong. All of them. Because what it's fundamentally like is just what it's like unfundamentally. Bloody confusion from start to finish."

A look of pain passed across David's face.

"Jesus, you're wrong," he said. "You must be wrong. Damn it all, the whole wisdom of - of civilisation, damn it, is against you. It's what they all say, not just the novelists, but the philosophers, the poets, the historians, the lot. That there is order underneath. A pattern. Or patterns. That in the end it makes sense. Oh, I know they each of them say it makes a different sort of sense, more or less. But they're all, really all, agreed that it does make sense at some level. It does."

"Then what sense does your great Conrad make of it? The horror, the horror? That it?"

"No. No, not at all. Oh, I wish you'd read the story. He doesn't say the horror, the horror. That's just pointing out there are more things in heaven and earth than poor old Mistah Kurtz, who's seen starting out as some sort of great civiliser, dreams of. The poor bugger goes jaunting into the Forest, begins by sending back scads of ivory, then meets some mysterious natives and goes pretty well bonkers and finally it's *Mistah Kurtz he dead.* Famous line. Which bloody Tom Mountjoy's entirely ignorant of."

"Well, if that's what the thing's about, if you ask me Conrad is saying it is all chaos and confusion. I'll join the club, like Reg."

"Reg? Reg, for God's sake. He thinks the Conrad books are just jolly adventure yarns. Which on the surface they are, some of them. But underneath they all are doing what I've said. Telling us what it's like, parts of it. All those tiny shifts of meaning that came on to the page as he wrote, the little differences that give academics such happy hours digging out... gave me, too, once. They add up to something. And in that story it isn't just *all's confusion, the horror, the horror.* It's the horror plus our ability to cope with it. Or to know how far away we are from coping with it. It's that and the universal greed, and man's inhumanity to man and a hell of a lot else."

"Okay, okay. But that's only one person's idea of what it's like. Why is Conrad so marvellous that we've got to accept it's the way he happens to say that it is?"

David relaxed.

"Oh, that's easy. All fictions have built into them a sort of fail-safe device. If they don't convince you about the world they show, they're not telling the whole truth. Not for you. Or not telling the whole truth about what they were trying to tell the truth about."

"So why not just try to find out for yourself? Why accept someone else's tidying-up? Even if they do happen to convince you?"

"Because, you idiot, those guys have been there before you, done the exploration. And they're people who've been granted insights. Insights that come from living through what they are writing about, even if they never move out of wherever it is they sit writing."

"Well, I don't buy it, that's all. If I'm going to find anything out, I'm going to find it out for myself."

David glared at her.

A minute of silence went by. Another. At the side of the boat below them the water of the river chuckled and gurgled as they thrust their way through it. Some small clumps of jacinthe d'eau floated past. Faraway to either side the high green walls of the Forest were dim and impenetrable.

At last something caught David's eye. He pointed.

"Look, a hippo. I swear that's a hippo over there."

Tom looked across without answering.

"Christ," David said, "I wish we'd bloody got there. Into the arms of Major Yombton-Smith."

***

Without M'bene's cheerful presence, Thomasina was finding Snail-Shell increasingly hard to put up with. When M'bene had been there, a respondent echo to the new way of life she had felt in herself from the moment she had elected in the attorney's office in Castle Street to make her expedition, she had had no difficulty in tolerating Snail-Shell's very different ways. But deprived of M'bene's insouciant approach to whatever befell them, good or bad, of his willingness to jump at risks, of his happy laughter, she soon began to be irked almost beyond endurance by the older man's obsessive caution.

Why, she thought almost every day and often more than once in a day, had she allowed Mr Sparrhawk to include him in her party?

She thought she knew what the American trader had seen in him. He had conceived the very cautiousness that so irritated her now as being necessary for her safety in the Forest. But, she said to herself, that caution is not really caution. It is not a calculation of risks. If it was that, she would perhaps have welcomed it from the start as a counterweight to M'bene's reckless impulsiveness. However much she felt in tune with that, she knew that it had its dangerous side. A check on it, for him, for her, would have been worth having. But Snail-Shell's actual rules-bound restraint was in fact a different matter, and an appallingly irksome one clogging her at every step forward.

Lying at night under the shelter of branches that kept off the rain which fell almost every day towards evening now, she was clearly aware that this caution of Snail-Shell's sprang only from an inability to act in any way differently from the ways he had learnt as a boy, hard though it was to imagine that set, grave face alight once with boyish mischief. No, the rituals and rhythms he had learnt in childhood had become so fixed in his mind that he was incapable of doing any single thing except through them.

In the days when M'bene had been leading them he had generally been jostled out of any full performance of those intricate rites he could hardly live without. He had resented that, she knew. But M'bene's cheerful dash had almost always swept that resentment aside. If Snail-Shell's insistence on some propitiatory ritual had begun to take up more time than M'bene could tolerate and he had set off on the march again with Fito and herself happy to accompany him, the old man could only abandon his rites half-completed and follow. Or be left alone in the Forest.

More than once she had thought that, locked in resentment, he was indeed going to stay behind on his own. But to decide to do that he would have needed to go through whatever prescribed observance he had learnt as a boy was appropriate. And there had never been time for that. So on each occasion he had come striding after them, a look of grumpy disapproval fixed on his face.

If the old fellow had once managed to elicit an answer from his consultation of tree, leaf, twig or animal spoor and had learnt that it was right for him to leave them, he would have had no difficulty existing on his own in the Forest. She knew that. Soon after setting out she had come to realise that his ceremonies, if not always logical, were at base tried and tested ways of relying on the Forest itself for safety, comfort and sustenance.

But now, increasingly, she herself was at the mercy of the rituals, however long they took, however wearisome they were, however lacking in logic they might be. So progress was always slower. And she felt fatigue dragging at her more with each successive day. Always, too, there was the burden of her guilt. And her doubts which with M'bene's death had returned in full force, the sense of oneness with the Forest she had attained in the aftermath of the storm that had sent the huge mahogany crashing almost on to her, washed altogether away.

The gusts of sharp fury Thomasina felt at Snail-Shell's encoiled caution, at his entrapment in the patterns he imposed upon himself, grew more and more frequent. They came to a head on the day that, in the middle of the narrow path they were following, the old man saw two large white feathers. They were lying in the softly slushy earth under the green gloom, each broken two or three times along its length. At the sight of them he had come to an instant halt.

Thomasina, controlling her irritation, asked what was the matter.

"Mauvais fétiche. Mauvais, mauvais."

Without further attempt at explanation, the old man stamped back past her. He eased his way in turn past the large frame of Fito, his burden, which included the Wardian case, on his head. Then, firmly presenting his back to both of them, he made it clear he intended to lead them off the way they had come.

It was then that Thomasina revolted.

The thought of any of the miles they had painfully traversed since morning being thrown away was more than she could endure. In the past few days every step she had taken had seemed to require a separate effort. It was, she knew, the effect of the fever she had suffered still lingering, but it was none the less wearisome for that. The rain too, that fell now with depressing regularity, had taken its toll on her lessened strength.

During the day the sun would send the occasional thin lively beam down through any break in the leaf-layer above, and the raindrops that had clung all night to twig and creeper would glint with sparkling brilliance. The tree shafts would be turned into grey graceful pillars, reaching up, up. The invisible birds above would pour out their repertory of amazingly varied songs and calls. Monkeys would swoop and swing in the wildest antics. And, exhilarated despite her fatigue, she would feel she could march on.

But as the day began to draw to its end, as it was doing now, all that animation would drain away. From the Forest. From herself.

Above, unseen, the clouds would have gathered, grey, rain-heavy and menacing. Then with perhaps a dull rumble of thunder the rain would begin its inevitable descent. There was no hope of shelter. Sooner or later the battering drops penetrated the layer upon layer of leaves above. Then they swiftly soaked every garment to the skin, warm at first, soon cold and clinging.

And now, simply because of the most trivial of circumstances, Snail-Shell was proposing to lose them heaven knew how many of the miles they had achieved. All for a couple of broken feathers.

"Non," she shouted. "Non. Nous continuons."

Snail-Shell stood unmoving. Even from the back of his stooped shoulders she could tell he was looking away down the path, his face set in determination. Fito, she saw, was torn between the two of them. He had begun, when he had seen what Snail-Shell intended, to go back. He never questioned the wisdom of the old man in Forest lore. But, at her sharp words, he had swung half-way back.

"Nous continuons," she said again, forcing herself to firmness.

"Danger," Snail-Shell muttered, not turning by so much as an inch. "Danger de mort."

Thomasina pointed a scornful finger at the two white feathers, more for Fito's benefit than Snail-Shell's.

"Danger?" she said. " Çela?"

"Grand danger de mort," Snail-Shell repeated, though making no attempt to say what precise *danger* he envisaged.

Thomasina gave a glare at his stubborn back of an intensity which, in distant, quiet Salisbury, she would not have believed lay within her.

"Fito, allons," she said.

She saw that now, at last, Snail-Shell had at least turned his head. A sudden hope possessed her that she was on the point of breaking the old man's sullen obstinacy. If M'bene could do it with his buoyant dash, he thought, what cannot I? There has been enough of this nonsense.

"Allons, Fito," she said once more.

Without giving so much as a quick glance to see whether she was being obeyed by either of the two, she strode straight over the feathers and marched steadily on.

But she listened.

She listened with all the acuteness of hearing that her time in the Forest had developed in her.

Almost at once she was able to detect Fito's tread, the tiny sounds of sodden twigs underfoot softly snapping. But, after him, was Snail-Shell following? As he had in the end always done when M'bene had thrust aside his interminable consultations of the Forest omens?

She walked on, head high.

Then, when she had gone some fifty yards, she heard from behind a single heavy thump. At once she knew what it was. Her sausage-like waterproof bag, Snail-Shell's burden of honour ever since M'bene's death. It had been hurled to the ground.

When at last she did turn it was to see, as she had known she would, Snail-Shell was nowhere in sight. He had departed. To be swallowed back into the Forest of which he had been no more than a part ever since the day of his birth.

***

Major Yombton-Smith, a frown of frank displeasure on his ruddy, snub-nosed face, stood in the middle of the large dumped assortment of expedition paraphernalia. Behind him, out in the river, the cargo boat lay, attended by its habitual flotilla of pirogues.

"I thought all arrangements had been made ex London," he said. "Full personnel included."

"Well, yes," Tom said, looking for the first time since she had been in Africa slightly abashed. "I know they were. But... well, we came across this fellow, N'goi, and he sounded as if he'd, well, make a useful cook."

"It was the way we came across him, really." David launched into explanation.

But a swift look from Tom stopped him adding anything more.

"Well," Major Yombton-Smith said, "dashed if I know what to do now. I mean, you've brought the chappie all the way here. He's definitely on your strength. But, on the other hand, I've commissioned a perfectly good cook myself. As per instructions."

"Yes," Tom said. "Yes, I know. But... well, couldn't we just take old N'goi along, and – and sort of see what happens."

"Hm? I must say I foresee some delicate problems there. Chain of command and all that..."

He scratched his head just above his right ear in what looked like a parody of thinking.

"No, I know," he said. "Change of plan. Nothing else for it. I'll leave my cook – call him cook A – here with Canopforce, and we'll take your chappie, cook B, with us. Avoid a nonsense that way."

"Canopforce?" David inquired, with an open touch of incredulity.

Tom gave him another quick glare.

"Fellows out here investigating the Forest canopy, scientists," the Major happily explained. "The chaps I've detached myself from to look after your team, Filmforce. I've designated you Filmforce, and they're Canopforce. Always helps with the paperwork."

"Filmforce, jolly good," Tom said, laying on the enthusiasm.

Major Yombton-Smith's ruddy face reddened yet more with pleasure. He bounced up and down two or three times in his calf-high safari boots.

"Yes, well, glad you've got here at last. I was afraid when you were adrift from your ETA that this chap Lunn would push off from camp Alcott. Made a quick recce up there a week ago, and he seemed pretty well a fixed point. But I formed the impression he's a bit of an unreliable bar-steward, if you'll forgive my French."

"Tell me about camp Alcott, Major," Tom said, almost fluttering her eyelids.

"Jacky. Jacky, dear lady. Always called Jacky."

"Well then, Jacky, what exactly is camp Alcott? I gather it's the only place we can be sure of meeting up with our Mr Lunn. But what is it?"

"Yes, well, interesting spot. In its way. Built by an American, name of Alcott, back in the 50's. Anthropologist. Studying the local tribe. Bringing some of them in from the Forest. Rest and recuperation, you might say. And for a time the place became a sort of tourist attraction.

But then old Alcott died, and the whole thing collapsed. It's pretty well a ruin now."

"Entropy," David was heard to mutter under his breath.

"And our prospector friend camps out there?" Tom said in a loud voice.

"From time to time, I gather. Yes. But, thing is, can he be relied upon to stay in situ till we make contact? If not, I can only say it'll be a damn poor show."

"Oh, yes, damn poor, damn poor," David said.

And this time Tom gave him a sideways kick. On the shin. And hard.

"So I'd like to be off there at first light tomorrow." Jacky Yombton-Smith said cheerfully, having apparently not noticed Tom's action.

"Track's pretty well motorable all the way," he went on, "and I've had two of Canopforce's spare vehicles fettled for you. So, oh six hundred hours kick-off, if that's all right by you?"

"Oh, yes. Yes, Major. Jacky. That'll be fine with us."

In the comparative privacy of the tent which Major Yombton-Smith had assigned to Tom – her name was on a piece of card pinned to the door-pole – David burst out.

"Fettled? Fettled? What in God's name does fettled mean?"

"I don't know. You're the one who's been to university, studied English. I suppose it means got ready. It's obvious really."

"Then why the hell can't he say got ready? Fettled. Fettled."

"Oh, Teigh, don't be a bore. The guy's alright really. Just a bit wrapped up in his military jargon."

"He's not alright. He's a sodding menace. Christ, Tom, we're going to be regimented off our feet. Kick-off at oh six hundred. Adrift from our ETA. And Filmforce. Filmforce, oh my God."

"All right, Filmforce is a bit much, I grant you, but –"

"And you. What about you? Filmforce, jolly good. Jolly good."

Tom's dark eyes blazed.

"I only said that because I could tell you were on the point of taking the piss out of the poor guy even more."

"Poor guy? The man's a maniac. Jesus, Tom, I don't think I can go through with this."

"Don't be bloody stupid. We've come all this way. We're in sight of our famous Tim Lunn. There's only the bit of rainforest left to do. There can't be any question of backing out now."

She calmed down a little.

"And besides," she added, "Jacky will get us there without any balls-ups. You can tell. And that's not to be sneezed at in Africa."

"Jacky. Oh, God, you're falling in love with him."

"Don't be fucking ridiculous. I can see what sort of an idiot he is as well as you. But he is efficient. So why not take advantage of that?"

"That's a fine new attitude. Explorer Mountjoy, stickler for good discipline and order."

"Oh, Teigh, just chuck it, will you? Yes, I do see the virtues of good discipline and order, if that's what you like to call it. They're going to make a hell of a difference to us here. I may have had another attitude back at home, but now I'm beginning to be thankful for anything that promises to go according to plan."

"Well, God help you, Tom Mountjoy."

***

Alone in the Forest with the strapping amiable Fito, Thomasina soon found the young man more talkative than he had been in all the weeks of their toilsome progress towards the object of her quest. She guessed that he had found impetuous boastful M'bene as intimidating as tradition-weighty Snail-Shell. Relieved of the presence of them both, he blossomed. She even learnt from him before long something he had not attempted to tell her in all the time she had known him. Fito was not, in fact, his name. It was a nickname jokingly bestowed on him by M'bene at the very start of their journey. A fito was a long supple sapling, particularly useful in hut building, and M'bene had called him that in reference to his height and his youth. She continued to use the name, however, especially as Fito seemed pleased with it coming from her.

It was only a few minutes after Snail-Shell had so dramatically let drop her long waterproof bag that Fito made the first considerable remark he had addressed to her in the whole course of their time together. As soon as they were certain that Snail-Shell was not going to appear out of the Forest again they had gone back together to retrieve the bag. Fito had slung it nonchalantly over his shoulder, seeming quite indifferent to the double weight of the bag and the box on his head. Then, when they had retraced their steps to the place where the feathers that had so disconcerted Snail-Shell lay, he had extended the toe of one foot to within an inch of them and had pronounced.

"Elles disent," he said, "on va nous tuer."

"Kill us? Rubbish," she had at once replied, robustly and in English.

A moment later she realised, with surprise, that this alone had been the effect that the threat of death had had on her. Still glowing with the rage that Snail-Shell's behaviour had warmed in her, she treated the threat as if it had been no more than the shouting of a rude boy in some street in Salisbury. And this despite the fact that she did not doubt for a moment that Fito had meant what he had said.

In any case, she thought, there is nothing else to do but to go on. Had there been some danger directly in front of her, the storm-terrified leopard, the ompenle snake that M'bene had killed, she would at once have sensibly backed away. But in the face of a nothingness she felt no inclination to retreat.

If Fito was right that the feathers had been placed where they were as a warning – and from the way Snail-Shell had behaved she had no doubt they were – then death might indeed come suddenly out of the green face of the Forest. A poisoned arrow. A spear thrust. Yet it was, somehow, hard to believe.

In the infinite confusion through which, confused, she was making her way it was just as possible that nothing would happen as that an arrow would fly or a man with a spear emerge. So to go on with her journey, deeper and deeper into the Forest, nearer and nearer to the end of the quest, to the triple waterfall and the plants that grew at its foot, was all there was for her to do.

She conveyed something of this to Fito. He smiled, shyly and ambiguously, but did not indicate in any way that he was unwilling to follow where she might take him.

It was less than an hour later that he abruptly spoke again.

"Village bientot. Ami moi."

She took in the words. So, they were coming to human habitation before long. It was likely enough. If those feathers had indeed been deliberately put on the path, then the path almost certainly lead somewhere. It would be a track that the inhabitants of this Forest-hidden village ahead were accustomed to take to go perhaps to a source of water, perhaps to somewhere where the hunting was good.

But there had been in Fito's brief announcement, she felt, a faint tinge of doubt. An *ami* he might have in this village, but he had not sounded altogether sure of the friendship. And earlier he had said, albeit cheerfully enough, *on va nous tuer*.

She would have liked to have discussed the precise meaning of the broken white feathers at more length. But communicative though Fito now was, the scantiness of the language they had in common put that out of the question.

So it was on into the unknown.

Before long a tapping tattoo on the leafy canopy overhead announced the arrival once again of rain. She shivered.

In a few moments, as the rain began to fall with its customary African violence, she was wet to her skin. Down Fito's slim brown back, as he strode ahead of her, rivulets ran.

She sneezed convulsively, once, twice, three times, four times.

Fito, turning a little, uttered what must have been his equivalent of "Gesundheit."

Tramping behind him slipping and sliding in the downpour, Thomasina found herself simply hoping she had not caught cold. Death might wait her. But the lesser evil seemed much more real. Her sentiments, she thought, were just those she would have had if she had been caught in a shower going from the cathedral to the house in the close without benefit of umbrella, though here she was positively wading through a miasma of grey water globules beating up from the earth as high as her waist.

Then, quickly as it had come, the rain ceased. Fito came to a halt in front of her, set down his two burdens and wrung out the cloth round his loins, without much regard for the proprieties.

Thomasina wished she could do as much.

Should she do so, she thought, take off blouse, skirt and underlinen and wring the rainwater out of them, Fito would doubtless pay as little attention as he had assumed she would pay to him. But years of enforced modesty were not so easily to be discarded.

Why, she recalled, even her mother, as soon as she herself had been old enough to look after herself in the bath, had withdrawn from the room before she had removed her petticoat. The notion was deeply implanted. Even the frequent sight of African women's bare breasts, familiar soon enough after her arrival in the Dark Continent though at first encounter they had produced in her a quiver of unease, had not overcome the reticences of a lifetime.

Sneezing still at intervals, her damp clothes clinging, she made her way onwards. The path at her feet steamed gently in the aftermath of the downpour. Odours, warm and fecund, rose up from it. She began to wonder if they should start looking about for somewhere to rest for the night.

But then, in the quiet after the passing of the noisy leaf-battering rain, she detected ahead unmistakable sounds of human activity. They were not sounds she had often heard since entering the Forest. Twice only, in fact, had their line of march brought them near to villages. But now, to judge by the feathers' warning, she had come to a part of the vast Forest where there were more human inhabitants. There must be not only the village ahead but other ones, whose peoples had to be kept at a distance.

Would she herself, and poor Fito, rank with those distrusted intruders? Were they really in *danger de mort*?

The sounds of activity grew louder. There was the hollow rhythmic tapping of someone beating out tree-bark to make cloth. There were shouts and the occasional laughter and screams of children. Soon she could distinguish the gossipy chatter of the women as they went about their work. From time to time came the deeper sound of men's voices. Then she smelt the tang of smoke from fires.

Fito, in front of her, went steadily onwards. Was he truly unconcerned at whatever reception they might get, she wondered. Or did he have so much faith in her own presence, a white woman, that he was indifferent to a danger that in other circumstances would have sent him round another way?

Then, suddenly as a trap-door apparition at the pantomime in Salisbury, two men stepped on to the path out of the vegetation to either side. They stood some ten yards distant, blocking the narrow track. Real men, not stage demons. Truly menacing. Their hostility so evident it could almost be smelt. They were armed, but not with the bow and arrows or spears she had half envisaged, but with short broad-bladed knives.

Fito let the sausage-bag slip from his shoulder to the ground. Then, slowly and carefully, he lowered the Wardian case down beside it. He did not put a hand near the machete at his waist, though Thomasina guessed he very much wanted to.

For moments that seemed to her long-drawn out beyond belief a tense silence quivered back and forth.

At last Thomasina snatched at a decision before licking cowardice might make her turn and run. Without making up her mind whether she was putting her trust in her evident womanliness, or on the necessarily strange appearance a white face must have, or merely on the power of sheer surprise, she stepped forward. Half a dozen paces took her almost right up to the two silent hostile presences. She halted then and pronounced, twice, a greeting-word she had earlier learnt.

"M'boloani. M'boloani."

Despite the African etiquette, of which she was also aware, that it was the men in possession who should hail the newcomer, one of the two forbidding presences before her at least answered with a grunt. But, beyond that, neither showed any less hostility.

Behind her, Fito, audibly swallowing, brought out the name of the *ami* he believed he had in the village beyond.

"Manyalibo."

There was no particular response. Minutes passed. If, in the Forest, minutes had any meaning.

Then, from further down the path, another man appeared. He was of middle age, well-built, leathery of face. He wore nothing but a twist of bark cloth round his middle and a knot of leopards' tails dangling from his shoulder.

"Manyalibo," Fito said.

There was a tinge of relief in his voice. And of doubt.

Manyalibo stepped between the two knife-carriers. Nothing in his expression showed either friendship or enmity. Or even, Thomasina thought, her heart abruptly racing, of appetite at the sight of killable meat.

Can that truly be, she asked herself. Can he be thinking of me at this moment as - as something to be eaten?

But it was possible, she thought. Here in the heart of Africa even that was possible.

Manyalibo came up to Fito.

Then he put out his two hands and held them, not touching, just above Fito's smooth-skinned shoulders. It was a greeting.

Thomasina, remembering seeing old Snail-Shell greet in this way a man he knew in the second of the two villages they had come to on their march, felt a wave of relief run down her from stiff spine to the curled toes in her boots.

CHAPTER 10

So there began for Thomasina a new period of her life, little though at the moment of stomach-loosening relief when the leathery-faced, powerfully authoritative Manyalibo had greeted Fito she had realised it. But, brought out perhaps by the shock of that confrontation, she proved almost at once to be on the point of succumbing, not to any English attack of the sniffles, but to a new worse bout of turmoiling fever.

Lying in a hut in the village, lost and wandering in a delirium far more raging and debilitating than the attack that had struck her down after M'bene's death, days and days went by for her in a swirl of nightmares and delusions.

All the while, fading and re-appearing, evasive as the acrid smoke that eddied from a clay pot beside her, she dimly recognised Manyalibo's leathery countenance and bunch of swinging leopards' tails.

It was Manyalibo who cared for her all during that time, though she mistook him more than once at the height of her fever confusion for old Doctor Tompstone. Doctor Tompstone, who had loomed over her bed in childhood measles, mumps and chicken-pox, a grey-whiskered kindness. Doctor Tompstone, who, in later years when her mother lay dying with black obscenities issuing from her lips, she had come to suspect of being nothing other than grey whiskers and ineffectual geniality.

But Manyalibo was not ineffectual. In all but the worst of her delirium and more as at last she began to recover, she recognised that. He brought her practical help at every stage. He forced into her mouth, at first against her will, concoctions - she never had any idea of what - that had soothed the worst of the fires that ran and jagged throughout her veins. Other remedies, later, brought down the fever little by little. Yet others began the process of strengthening her exhausted body.

It was because of this care, she later reflected, that it had been only Doctor Tompstone who had appeared to her in the delusions of delirium. When she was able to think, lying in a state of lazy torpor, she wondered why it had been that the figures of admonitory Mr Sparrhawk and, yet more, palely intense Père Jossuet had not come to haunt and vex her. She came to the conclusion eventually that it was somehow Manyalibo's authoritative and reassuring presence that had warded off all that was fearful.

And Manyalibo did more for her. When she was lucid, though still too weak to do anything other than lie in the leaf-shaded stillness of the hut, he talked to her. So, almost without knowing it, she acquired the curious, tone-varying language of her hosts. Before the days when, with Manyalibo at her elbow, a gaunt but sympathetic presence, she took her first few tottering steps outside she had enough of a grasp of the tongue that there was nothing in the simple talk of the village that she could not understand.

Then, as day by day she grew stronger, a whole new world presented itself to her.

It was at first no more than the little society of the village itself. On her first two encounters with Forest dwellings, months earlier when cheerful impulsive M'bene had been her guide, she had gained, she now saw, only the most cursory view of the life led in them. She had thought it was crude, almost at the level of the farmyard, but now she became aware, quickly enough, of a complexity she had had no idea of, though it was a complexity that needed few words for its conduct.

Her awareness had begun, in fact, before she had reached the stage of being well enough to leave the bed of softly springy branches on which she had worn out her fever. One day then she had heard Manyalibo say to his wife, who was helping him in his nursing of her, that she herself was "dead".

For one terrible moment, in her weakness, she had thought it must be true.

Was she dead? Had she in fact expired? Was it only her spirit, hovering there, that had heard the words exchanged between the two of them?

But at once, despite her weakness and wandering state, she had thrown off the will-o-the-wisp notion. No, by heavens, ill she might be, but dead she was not.

She said as much at once to Manyalibo. She even reached, in the heat of the repudiation she felt, something of the assertiveness of her days of health. Immediately Manyalibo explained what he had meant, though clearly he found it hard to understand the notion of death that she had herself. You did not die all at once, Manyalibo said. If the Forest was not kind towards you, to begin with you might be merely too hot. Next you might have fever, such as she herself had had and was hardly yet free from. After that you became ill, as she had been when she had first come. After being ill, unless the Forest could bring you back, you became dead. She was dead now, or perhaps had been until this moment. Luckily she had escaped becoming completely dead, a state which almost always led to being dead for ever. When anyone was dead for ever it was necessary to bury their body.

She had found it all hard to grasp. It was almost as difficult for her as it had been for Manyalibo to believe that anyone, even someone as strange and distant as herself, could think that you were either well or dead for ever. But, lying in the cool dimness of the hut pondering, she did begin at last to feel she had grasped the thought.

Perhaps now, she said to herself, I am getting near to being able 'to think black'. She recalled Mr Sparrhawk, lean and stringy in his striped cotton trousers and with his little goatee beard, as he strode up and down the veranda of his trading-post explaining to her the concept he felt to be vital to the understanding of the inhabitants of the Dark Continent. Was she now at last grasping the notion Mr Sparrhawk had found so hard to put into words, the feelings-thought he claimed distinguished the African mind from the white man's? In logic, in the logical way in which she and all Europeans were brought up to think, certainly you were either alive or dead. But, if you did not attempt to go by logic – difficult though it was to put oneself into that frame of mind – then was it not possible to conceive of experiencing a feeling being in succession hot, fevered, ill, dead, completely dead and soon to be dead for ever?

But, to her surprise, when she was able to go about in the village, welcoming on her exhausted limbs the strengthening influence of the sun that poured into the village clearing, it was not feelings-thought she found all about her but every evidence of logic and order.

Nowhere was this more so, to her recovering mind seeing everything about her as though she were new-born, than in the work of making baskets and the long nets used for hunting. These tasks Manyalibo had instructed her – he had, she thought, a good deal in him of the schoolmaster – were ones that fell to women. To men it fell to hunt, to bring meat from the Forest or honey or fruit from the tall trees. She translated what he had said to her in those terms, 'it fell to'. But she knew that Manyalibo meant more than this. The different tasks were what the Forest, in breeding women and men, had bred in them.

In that, she saw, a degree of order, a dictate of order, that till then it had never occurred to her that there could exist among any community of savages. And, more, she came to see, too, in the actual making of net and basket another affirmation of orderliness. From the tangled wildness growing all round them the women took stick and vine and put them into shapes of regularity. Simply and without fuss, they wrenched order out of chaos.

Watching the women make for her a hut of her own now that she was well enough not to need constant attention, she saw sticks of the right length and suppleness – fitos, in fact – thrust into the ground at exact intervals. As soon as enough of them were in place more pliant twigs were laced through them, again at exact intervals. Only when this stage of the simple construction had been reached did she appreciate why those intervals were as they had been made. They corresponded, precisely, to the width and length of the big mongongo leaves that made the covering of the hut, lapped neatly as tiles or slates, to form a rainproof skin. Even in the cutting of the big heart-shaped leaves, she saw, precision had been needed. Each stalk had been chopped across at an exact distance from the base of the leaf. In this way enough stalk was left on the leaves to use to make firm hooks to hold them in place in the rows of pliant stick that formed the frame.

It was a principle not spelt out in any book of rules or in some neat algebra primer but in the work of the hut-makers' hands. They were hands, she saw as she sat in the shade on a chair made for her from a bundle of sticks, that worked without any overseer. The women seemed all to know just what had to be done. The work sprang from their lives. And it was a work of order-bringing.

Much of this same unexpected orderliness in this lost little cluster of humanity deep in the Forest – there were no more than thirty-five or forty people in it all told – showed itself to Thomasina's newly-opened eyes in its daily activities.

She saw the women emerge from the huts every morning at first light and make their way to the little river not far away to fill their pots with water. She saw them cook the morning meal, unfailingly in the same manner, and take the men's share to them where they sat in an isolation that appeared to have been decreed without decree. She saw the women set out for their regular collection of firewood. She saw them tending the fires with scrupulous cunning. Only when Manyalibo told her that they had no means of generating fire and had to keep some embers alight from the gift lightning had brought them at some time in the forgotten past did she realise how vital was the ordered care the women brought to that task. Even, he said, when the time came to move the village to wherever better food supplies were to be garnered from the Forest a glim of fire had to be carried with them, wrapped in leaves known not to burn.

All this and more, day by day under Manyalibo's tutelage, she came to learn. And to wonder at.

Today for the first time I do not know for how long, for how many days, for how many weeks, I put pencil to paper. I have been ill, very ill. And I have been succoured. How extraordinarily so I still can hardly believe. At one moment, it seems to me now looking back, I was tramping with my amiable Fito through a particularly thick-growing area of the Forest, feeling what I believed was merely the onset of a nasty cold and concerned, too, though but vaguely, at the possibility of encountering hostile savages of cannibalistic persuasion. Then at the next moment, after that encounter had as I believed taken place – it had such an air of the unreal that it might have been pure hallucination – I was lying in such security as I could hardly credit after so long amid the uncertainties of the Forest. I was ill, yes, ill almost unto death, but I was nurtured. And it is to one Manyalibo that I owe that security.

One hour later. It is to Manyalibo, too, that I owe the interruption. He had not seen my memoranda books or my pencil until this day. He had not seen me writing. Indeed – and this I find hard to comprehend still – had never seen anyone performing the act of writing until an hour ago. He had no idea what I was doing, and I have had the greatest difficulty explaining it to him. True, it did not take him long to grasp the notion that marks on paper could represent the words he was accustomed to say, though I verily believe he had not until this time thought of what he said as being made up of 'words'. They were his thoughts that he spoke aloud. But quickly enough, for he is the soul of intelligence, he made the transition from his previous notion of thoughts voiced to that of there being words that could be set apart. From that it was no difficulty for him to understand that these words could be represented by some marks made on paper with a pencil much like the designs in the black juice from some nut that I have seen the women and girls of the village make upon each others' bodies by way of decoration. How for a moment I was shocked to witness for the first time the particular care one young lady was lavishing upon the posterior of another sprawled across her lap. Yet, after a little reflection, I was able to see how much a matter of course that was, no different from the sewing of ribbon or braid on to the skirt which covers that portion of one's own anatomy.

I digress. Manyalibo's difficulty concerning my putting pencil to paper was over an altogether more fundamental matter, and one which, in my happy ignorance, it had never occurred to me in all my twenty nine years as being something to be questioned. Why, Manyalibo quite simply asked me, was I engaged in this curious business, writing? He had to use the English word I had used myself to describe the act, it is so far from anything anyone in his world had conceived of. It came out as "N'ritey" as well as I can set it down, but we understood one another to perfection. And I understood, too, that he had set me a poser, a question infinitely more difficult to answer than any Miss SixSmith ever put in her examinations. Why do I engage in the business of n'ritey? Why do I commit these words to these pages? I can no longer tell myself they are here for my dear Doctor Diver's benefit.

He is dead, dead for ever, as Manyalibo would say, and I have to acknowledge that I have been cheating myself, why I cannot quite tell, in setting down my thoughts as if they were for his eyes. So why, in truth, in very truth have I been doing this thing?

What eventually I told Manyalibo, though with all his intelligence I am not sure that in the end he fully understood – or that I did myself – was that in some way committing an account of my activities to paper makes them more real to me. I feel when I have written of them that they have been truly done, that they have been redeemed from the flux and fixed for all time. And, indeed, so strange have been some of the things that have fallen to my lot since I have been in Africa, events seemingly belonging to the confusion and fantasy of the world of dreams, that I might well feel I needed to turn back to these pages and read to convince myself that those events had really happened. That I, Thomasina le Mesurier, spinster of the parish of St Martin, in Salisbury, Wiltshire, had attempted to befriend a black madman more than six feet in height, that this same Thomasina le Mesurier came face to face with an enraged leopard at the height of a tornado storm of such ferocity that no one in happy England would believe it, that I, alas, alas, have witnessed the death of one M'bene, faithful friend and servitor, and have admitted to myself that to an extent his death lies at my door – all this I might cease to believe had happened were it not set down in words in this my water-worn journal with this my increasingly small stub of indelible pencil (others I have, however, and will not fail to use).

So to Manyalibo I said that writing things down gave them more reality. But, of course, I could not use that word 'reality', and my fumbling attempts to convey what I meant foundered hopelessly. "It is what happened?" Manyalibo had asked me. "Yes." But, he said, it has happened, it has gone. He shrugged his shoulders then, making his knot of leopards' tails, sign of his prowess as a hunter, jig up and down. It was as much as to say, though he did not have the words to explain an idea that seemed beyond my comprehension, that when a thing has gone it has gone. It is no more. I suppose he would say, if he had been able to realise that I needed to have it said to me, that it is worth remembering anything of tangible advantage, in what tree last year a bees' nest was found so that the place can be visited again, at what time some particularly fine fruit comes to ripeness, but that anything else that has happened and will not happen again is not worth remembering if you do not happen to remember it. Beyond that he will not go. But for myself I feel still that to set down in writing the events that I have experienced begins somehow to show me

117

a pattern. The setting-down makes for sense. And sense I must have.

But I do not think Manyalibo requires any more sense than that which the Forest provides for him day by day.

CHAPTER 11

When Thomasina had recovered enough of her strength Manyalibo began taking her into the Forest. She had labelled him in her mind as a schoolmaster, and her feeling had been right. Savage from the heart of the African jungle he might be, she had thought once, but put all the world into the categories appropriate to them and he was, through and through, a schoolmaster. Where he saw ignorance he wanted to teach.

There was one aspect of his life, however, she had found hard at first to associate with the schoolmasters she had known in Salisbury, her father's friends, occasional visitors to his widow. When at last she had been able to leave her sick-bed and had begun to take in the life of the little village it had been borne in on her that Manyalibo's wife who had helped to nurse her, a bright-eyed person of much his age by the name of Kondabate, was not his only wife. He had another, of much the same age, called Sau, more of a stay-at-home, for ever busy with some task. But – and this had given her a dart of pure dismay when she had realised it – he also had a third wife, a young and very pretty girl, Asofalinda.

The whole arrangement led her to much perplexed thought as she rested outside the hut that had been built for her. First, it struck her watching what went on in the village clearing that all Manyalibo's wives were happy. True, there were occasional little differences between them. But, she soon realised, these were of just the same sort as the petty disputes that sometimes had taken place between the servants at home, differences her mother or herself had easily been able to iron out if they had not subsided of themselves. They had done nothing to detract from the real harmony of their household, and neither did the moments of dispute in Manyalibo's establishment.

Next she became aware of something else that, to her great surprise, did not seem to cause disruption in Manyalibo's hut.

When habitations are made of nothing more sturdy than mongongo leaves, however neatly arranged, she found, there were no barriers to sounds at all. So from her hut, lying awake at night listening to the ordinary noises of the Forest, the pink-pink-pink of frogs, the grunts of warthogs, the despairing rasping call of the rock-badger, she was also very much aware of other sounds. Manyalibo, she discovered, despite the difference in age between himself and pretty little Asofalinda, had long periods of patent pleasure in her arms, her evidently very ready arms.

Squeals, chuckles, gasped words, slaps, pealing laughter, screeches, giggles, both feminine and masculine, and eventually ever more intense moans of pleasure made it all too clear to her what was happening in the rich darkness of the next-door hut.

Twisting uneasily on the entwined twigs of her bed, never till now uncomfortable beneath her, the exchanges produced in her an aching censoriousness. This is the blind, thoughtless, all-or-nothing happiness of the world-forgetting lotus-eater, she told herself. It has nothing of the reasoned bliss of a Christian marriage, as I used always to understand it should be.

Then she would think of Manyalibo's other two wives, as aware as herself, more so, of what was happening. She marvelled at their acceptance of it, and found it hard indeed to understand.

It was only when, out one day with Manyalibo, the schoolmaster personified, she learnt from him something about the variety of mating patterns in the Forest that she began to see him and his wives with new eyes.

She had been engrossed in his showing her what in the tracks left by a little deer indicated the ideal place to set a snare-net when she was startled by an extraordinarily plaintive musical cry coming from some point she could not make out in the leaf canopy above. It was answered at once by a similar cry from a slight distance away, as hauntingly beautiful.

She thought the sounds must be those of a pair of birds she

had never before heard calling. But, when in a whisper, she asked Manyalibo what they were – he, too, had stood intently listening – he told her that, no, they were the calls of a pair of apes, very rarely heard, almost never seen. They were called kooloos.

When it was certain that the creatures had moved on out of hearing Manyalibo told her more about them. A kooloo, he said, mated with only one other kooloo, and, once chosen, the pair stayed linked to one another their whole lives. More, the calls she had heard were those of this pair of kooloos and no others. They arrived at the exact nature of them between themselves, and they kept them as long as they were together. In this they were unlike any other ape or monkey in the Forest.

Thomasina was very well aware of the random copulations of the big black-and-white monkeys that abounded everywhere, and of the same behaviour among all the others she had seen. At first she had averted her eyes from such blatant couplings, though she had long since become accustomed to the sight. But Manyalibo's account of the kooloos' life gave her food for deeper thought.

Later that day she wrote in her journal "*I cannot truly see why the world should be so ordered that it is one man, one wife everywhere and in all circumstances.*" She could see, then, that if the kooloos set an example of fidelity that would not have shamed a story of ancient chivalry, Manyalibo's three wives were equally content with their mode of existence. Their shared husband, it was plain, seemed to them as much in the order of things as, to her parents, monogamy had seemed the only way life could be lived.

But the next time she committed more of her thoughts to her memoranda book she reverted to the subject of the kooloos, though on a different note. She was, she wrote, in all probability the only white person ever privileged to have heard that extraordinarily beautiful ape converse. That was not unlikely, she reflected looking up from her page of neat purplish writing. There was so much in the tumultuous life of the vast stretches of the Forest that the existence of a whole species could well go unknown. The existence of the kooloos could, indeed, easily go unrecorded for hundreds of years to come, had she not heard it that single time.

She dropped her pencil into her lap then, and laughed aloud.

What was she, Manyalibo's hugely ignorant pupil, doing making a claim of that sort? Had not Manyalibo heard the ape calls? Long before they had ever come to her ears, too? And he had known what lives the apes led. That he must have learnt from his ancestors, reaching back through the ages. A fine pioneer she was.

Yet, she thought, back in England she would very likely write a paper for the *Annals and Magazine of Natural History* on the kooloo ape and its way of life. If ever she did return to England.

For the second time since that day in the attorney's office in Salisbury she saw her expedition no longer as a triumph, accident apart, that was bound to come. She doubted suddenly, more clearly than she had done in her fever after M'bene's death, the hard-won path she had always envisaged, to the place where Doctor Diver's plant grew, to its capture, its careful transport back through the Forest to Boma and the steamer to Liverpool. She ceased then to see those clover-leafed plants being tended and increased in the botanic gardens at Kew. She lost sight of the renown she had believed always would come at last to her old dear dead friend and of the benefits that humanity would gain. Instead she saw herself – but it was momentarily only – as a prisoner of the Forest. A curiously willing prisoner of a world that embraced both the rioting monkeys and chaste kooloo.

A moment later she had shaken herself vigorously and snapped her memoranda book shut. Sharply she put that fancy down to the last lingering effects of her illness. Or perhaps she owed it, she thought, to Manyalibo's influence on her. He was possessed, she had felt more than once before, of a mysterious power. Or was it perhaps the power of the Forest itself? Something she did not know whether she welcomed or profoundly distrusted?

Stickily entwined with Tom under the mosquito net, David suddenly rolled away.

"Old Thomasina," he said, "taking on board polygamy, pretty well just like that. That diary entry where she says "*I cannot truly see why the world should be so ordered that it is one man, one wife everywhere and in*

122

all circumstances." Not bad for a Victorian spinster, into her thirties, brought up in a cathedral close, when you come to think of it.'

"You, however – however – were meant to be thinking of something else."

"Christ. Yes, I know. Sorry. Sorry."

He made a move to clamber back.

"Don't bother. If you're so little interested you take time off for historical reflection, then I'm sure I can manage quite happily without."

"No, but - oh God, I have said I'm sorry. It was... it was just that the actual circumstances, well, it sort of put me in mind of Thomasina and polygamy and monogamy. All that. Monogamy mostly."

"Fucking sod it, I believe you were bloody going to suggest getting married once again."

Chastened, David sneaked out and headed back to the tent Major Yombton-Smith had assigned to him. On his way back to his own carefully labelled tent, he happened to notice the flap of Major Yombton-Smith's tent had been left open and he could see within a small trestle table with a paraffin lamp lighting a stack of paper next to an ancient typewriter. His curiosity piqued, he ventured towards the tent, looking round to make sure he wasn't observed. He listened carefully but could hear no sound coming from within. Holding his breath, he peeped inside, desperately trying to come up with a made-up query should he find the Major within.

No excuse was necessary however as the tent was deserted. Quickly David went over to the table and started reading the page in the typewriter with the heading 'Diversionary Tactics'. It appeared to be some kind of record of the Major's time in Africa. Despite the risk of being caught prying, he could not help but swiftly scan the other sheets of manuscript that lay beside the typewriter. Skipping to the bottom of the pile he came across Chapter 12 'Film Force'. Fascinated, he started to read an account in typical military style of his despair at having to cope with people of an artistic temperament.

Before he had got very far down the page he heard a distant rustle of leaves and – was it his imagination? – a footfall. Whatever the sound had been, it was enough to spook him and he quickly restacked the manuscript and left the tent.

***

Under Manyalibo's tutelage Thomasina was taught more than she had ever been able to imagine about the laws and usages of the Forest. Patiently he made her read deeply in what she came to think of as the book of vines and creepers.

She learnt, as she had not done with Snail-Shell, traditionalist in Forest lore, to recognise not just one or two useful lianas but an immense variety of them and to know the uses to which they could be put. There was one so extraordinarily supple that she, with her small hands, was easily able to wrap it round any object, yet which had the strength of a hawser. There was another that combined just the right amount of elasticity with stiffness to make it something that might have been designed by an engineer for hauling objects as heavy as a tree-trunk needed to bridge a stream. There was the creeper – split it revealed a bright yellow interior – that could be cut into bandage-like strips to bind loads for carrying.

For each purpose, it began to seem to her, there was a liana uniquely suitable. This was a lesson she learnt at some cost to herself.

At times she had found herself wishing a little that her Forest tutor would remember that she was of something more than schoolroom age. Then, one day in the Forest, while she had been deliberately absenting herself from his schoolmasterly eye she felt the ground beneath her feet suddenly give way and a moment later she was lying, bruised but no worse, at the bottom of a game-pit. Dug at the bounds of the village's acknowledged territory by their nearest neighbours, this was a trap impossible to extricate oneself from. It was bottle-shaped in construction, and its sides were lined with downwards-pointing spikes of sharpened wood.

Well aware of her foolishness and repentant somewhat of the pique that had got her into the difficulty, there was nothing she could do but call Manyalibo for help. He came with all the promptness she could have wished. Looking down at her with only the smallest air of rebuke on his leathery face, he told her he would go and fetch the very vine needed to haul her out.

He was away for an hour. Or for what Thomasina, who had long before ceased winding the stout silver watch recommended by Mr Galton, felt to be a full hour. The length of the absence so infuriated her that, once up on the ground again, she delivered a sharp attack on her rescuer.

"There is one vine only that will pull up such a weight as yours and keep you clear of the spikes," Manyalibo said. "I had to go far to find it."

It was during one of these intricate lessons of his that, out of the blue, she recalled what she had read about lianas during her preparations for coming to Africa. The author of a treatise she had borrowed from the Royal Geographical Society divided lianas according to the shapes they grew in. There were the straight, the looped, the thorn-covered, the reniforms, the falciforms, the luniforms. In her first days in the Forest she had been delighted when she had spotted, not without difficulty in the confusion of vegetation all round, a cluster of kidney-shaped creepers or a sickle-shaped one or, prize capture, the half-moon shape. Those classifications amid the chaos, she thought now, were compared with Manyalibo's no more than the play of an infant with a set of coloured wooden bricks.

More, Manyalibo's knowledge of Forest ways was practical as well as minute. As day by day she regained her fever-sapped strength she learnt from her schoolmaster how to tease termites from their almost impregnable hard earthen mounds in the way the chimpanzees did with a fine stick. She learnt, too, to distinguish between soldier termite and worker termite and which made the better eating. How far, she thought now, she had come from that day when her stomach had nearly revolted at a meal of snake.

She learnt not only which insects were good to eat – there was a kind of caterpillar that, threaded on a stick and roasted, was particularly delicious – but which were dangers prudently to withdraw from. It was when she had almost regained her full strength that, out in the Forest, Manyalibo abruptly drew her attention to the noisiness that had sprung up in the stilled hush. She realised then that animals were making their way at speed through the vegetation, suddenly careless of what predators they might attract. Insects flew past. Other creatures she saw making their way along the ground, seemingly in panic. A snake slid swiftly by, so close to her that she could have trodden on its head.

At first she thought there must be some huge fire somewhere. But she could smell nothing. But Manyalibo was gripping her arm and tugging her off in the direction the running creatures were taking.

Breathlessly she asked what was happening. Ants, Manyalibo replied. Then it was that she recalled what she had read about the driver ants of the Forest, a phenomenon she had not till now chanced to come across.

Manyalibo propelled her along until at last they came to the stream where the women of the village drew water. Without more explanation, he dragged her into it until they were standing four or five yards from the bank with the water up to their waists. Then he explained.

Ants of this sort moved, he said, as if they were not thousands and thousands of individuals but as one, like a snake.

But that snake, though only a hand's-breadth wide, could be so long that it might take from sunrise to sunset to pass. Any living thing that could not get out of its way was doomed; vicious jaws by the hundred seized its flesh. Tiny piece after tiny piece was tugged out and devoured. A deer might be left a bare skeleton within the time it took to sing one song. Even the leopard fled before these tiny creatures. Birds in their nests at the top of any small tree were not safe. The snake-army would climb to the top, devour, climb down again and march, march.

That night she wrote in her journal. "*I felt that such an army, devoted to a single object, as they might be Hannibal's soldiers making the crossing of the Alps with their elephants, must have a general. Manyalibo tells me that it is not so. He has seen these columns on the march often and knows that, far from coming under the command of any single individual, even the larger ants that stand at the column's sides and might seem to be its 'officers' are no such thing. They are*

126

the soldiers only. Their task is to defend. Even the great queen ant, big with eggs, that may sometimes be seen being carried, palanquin-like, by the onward marching column is no Boadicea. Her task in life is to lay those eggs, to provide the new generation. She, like her soldiers, like her onward-flowing workers, is at the call of some deep force that causes this terrible march to occur. Manyalibo says that this is the Forest. If he is right, then I fear its fearful order is chaos itself."

It was another, much less horrifying phenomenon that produced some days later further reflections in her memoranda book.

Butterflies, this time, were the subject of Manyalibo's lesson.

He showed her a length of vine that had fallen from one of the giant trees under whose leafy shade they wandered. On it were – a rare sight in the gloom – a dozen huge butterflies, brilliant in colour, hovering over the liana's flowers, still unfaded as jewel-bright almost as the butterflies over them. These fluttering creatures were, Manyalibo said, the sole ones able to survive the poison in this particular vine's leaves. Their caterpillars, feeding on the poisonous leaves, became impregnated with the poison themselves and all the birds had learnt not to take them.

"The colour warns them," he said.

The butterflies, he went on to explain, discovered whether or not they had located this vine by alighting on its leaves and 'making a sound like drums, but small, small, with their legs. Only this vine produced the particular sound they recognised. Thomasina marvelled. But her tutor had more to tell her. Since no butterfly would lay its eggs where another had already laid some so as to give the caterpillars that would emerge from them a free pasture, the vine contrived to grow here and there little clumps that exactly resembled the butterfly's eggs. In that way, he said, the vine prevented too many caterpillars from eating its leaves. So it lived on.

He showed her a clump of the false eggs. She found she could not brush them from the leaf. But, when he found for her a cluster of eggs he said were those of the butterfly, at a touch they were scattered.

"Mr Darwin appears to have the right of it," she wrote that evening. *"I begin to realise he has seen deeper than Manyalibo, deep though I feel my 'schoolmaster' has seen. There is an order to be taken out of all the piled-up*

confusion. There is a reason behind it all. That species of butterfly has lived on year after year because it learnt long ago not to eat those poisonous leaves. It gave itself its own bright colour because, in time, that stood as a sign to the birds to refrain from pecking it up. The vine, too, learnt to protect its leaves by creating those false eggs so that it could live long enough to form seed, to scatter it and thus perpetuate itself amid the Forest's wild struggle. Yes, there is an order."

***

Major Yombton-Smith took his eyes for a moment from the track as their vehicle bounced along between the springing-up growths of secondary forest to either side.

"Gosh," he said, "how marvellous it is out here, miles from anywhere, area largely devoid of human beings."

After a moment Tom found a reply.

"You don't much care for people then, Jacky?"

"Oh yes, old girl. I mean, damn it, in the army one's jolly close to one's brother officers, day in, day out. And to one's men. Pulling together as a team, you know. That's what it's all about."

"But all the same," David, sitting just behind, probed, "you like the primev- you like the Forest, devoid as it is of humans largely?"

"Yes."

Jacky Yombton-Smith thought for a little, expertly guiding the vehicle past the bumps of tree roots and the deep puddle holes.

"Bit of contradiction there, I suppose," he said eventually. "But that's the way it is. Might mention that in my book."

"Book?" Tom said innocently exchanging a conspiratorial glance with David.

Jacky Yombton-Smith's ruddy face went a deeper shade of russet.

"Spoke a bit out of turn there," he said. "Didn't want to mention my literary aspirations. Not in front of artistic types like you, begging your pardon."

"No need," David answered. "No need at all. So what is this book to be about Major?"

"Oh, sort of log of my time in the rainforest, you know. Just that.

Thought it might be of some interest."

"Jacky, I'm sure it would," Tom said ignoring a prod from David. "Fascinating."

"Glad you see it that way. After all, it is fascinating really, isn't it? The rainforest. Here. Miles from civilisation. All that."

"So what are you going to say about us?" David put in. "two artistic types lost in the jungle."

"Well, I don't think you are exactly lost. I mean, I've got my bearings okay, and you're with me."

He fell silent for a little. Then he looked up from the road ahead again.

"Actually," he said, "I hadn't thought you'd somehow come in. I mean, it's what Canopforce is doing here that's really interesting, isn't it?"

"Oh, yes," David agreed with every indication of sincerity.

Again Jacky Yombton-Smith was silent. And again after a little he spoke.

"Though, of course, I might have space for a sort of – what d'you call it – digression. Yes. If, of course, my scribbling ever see the light of day."

***

Thomasina found herself torn between two opposing desires. The more she learnt from Manyalibo the more she found herself possessed of a longing to acquire yet more insights into that library to which she had once compared the Forest. On the other hand, she found she had not, now that her fever and its effects were fully thrown off, lost the ambition that in the attorney's office in Castle Street in Salisbury, had launched her into Africa. She would find that plant Doctor Diver had once been in possession of – Manyalibo, when she had asked him if he knew of it, had said that he had never seen it or the place where she thought it grew – and she would take it back, over every obstacle, to the civilised world. She would vindicate her old friend, and herself.

She said nothing of this ambition to Manyalibo, however. For one thing, she doubted if she would be able to explain to him deeply intelligent though he was, a notion far removed from his own world. And, for another thing, she had so far been unable to make up her mind between the two courses, the two lives, that seemed to lie before her. The battle between them, she felt, must be conducted on the field of her own mind.

However strong in her that desire was to finish the task she had set herself, to bring that healing plant to restore order in time of plague, she was yet deeply grateful that the chance of the fleeting friendship young Fito had once had with Manyalibo had brought her to him. No one else, she thought, could have taught her as much as he had done about the Forest and given her the opportunity – terrible temptation – of plunging into it to learn more.

And terrible that temptation was. She could see herself, under its spell, learning and learning not only more facts about the multifarious Forest but acquiring, too, a feeling for its life. Was this, she asked herself once as she let that battle rage in her mind, was this the evil Père Jossuet had warned her of? Somehow the cool spirit of inquiry that Manyalibo had fostered in her did not seem to equate with the vague but intense evil the priest had conjured up for her. But the lure of the Forest, of the Forest alone in the purity of its being, was certainly a force that exerted an attraction that was beyond any outward pleasure of mere curiosity satisfied or half-satisfied. It was a new force battling in her mind to win for the Forest a final ascendency. It was towards the end of the season for honey – Forest luxury – and, for no particular reason, she learnt abruptly then how it was that Manyalibo himself had come to acquire his own immense knowledge of the Forest and its ways.

It was the sight of Fito clumsily and harmlessly flirting with Manyalibo's pretty Asofalinda that brought it about. Quite suddenly the old schoolmaster began to tell her his story. He, too, he said, had in youth been a great one for talking to women. But this inclination – to Thomasina's head there came for an instant the sounds she would hear at night from the hut where Manyalibo and Asofalinda lay – had played a trick on him. He had fallen totally in love with the wife of one of the other men of the village. It was against all custom. It had even been against his own wishes. "I was young, I wanted only to be as the others. But it happened. The Forest turned away from me, I was bad."

He glanced across to where Asofalinda sat working a strip of bark to smoothness on her plump and beguiling thigh. Fito beside her was laughing. But, Thomasina noted with relief, Manyalibo showed no sign of jealousy.

The other man's wife of Manyalibo's youth, however, he had told her, had given her husband every cause for jealousy. She had allowed herself to be seduced. Not once, but time after time.

Listening to Manyalibo gravely telling her the story of his young days, Thomasina recalled, as if from another planet, a similar event that had disturbed quiet cathedral life when she had been a girl of seventeen. She had never learnt any details, not even the name of the man involved. The lady was a certain Mrs. Watson, whom she found it hard to think of as a scarlet woman if only because she herself taught her two little daughters in Sunday school. All she had ever known of the scandal was in the nature of an atmosphere. There would be abrupt lapses in the conversation when she happened to enter a room. There had been murmured words sometimes about 'the seventh commandment.' Her two little pupils had suddenly ceased to come to her classes, and there had been no explanation. Nothing else. Simply a hiatus in the pattern.

But here in the Forest she was not only hearing the details – it never occurred to Manyalibo not to talk of them in full – of an affair essentially similar, but she was accepting them as something that had simply happened. A thwacking, twisting strand of disturbance had run through the little society of Manyalibo's youth, and she was hearing of it.

It had not been long, Manyalibo had continued, before it had become plain to all that more than a single lapse had occurred. The proper pattern of things was being wantonly broken. So he had been set upon by the husband and by all the men of the village. He had been whipped out of it.

"Look," he said, turning his back towards Thomasina. "Look hard at me."

She peered closely at his tough-skinned bare back with the knot of leopards' tails dangling beside it. Faint but unmistakable, she saw what she had never hitherto noticed. Like the tracks left in the wet by some little snake, across and across, there were the scars of that whipping long ago.

"So I stayed in the Forest," Manyalibo said. "Alone."

Thomasina could understand, to an extent, the force of that word 'alone'. Men from the village went often enough on their own into the Forest to hunt. But such wanderings never lasted beyond the day. On one occasion when one of the young bachelors had not returned by the time the sudden darkness fell there had been consternation in the whole village. Search parties had gone out with flaring torches, calling loudly in the dark, until at last the young man, who had fallen from a tree and hurt himself, had been found.

So for Manyalibo to stay in the Forest on his own was a great rent in the pattern. But then his extraordinary passion of desire had been an equal repudiation of the expected.

"How long did you stay outside the village?" she asked.

"For four years."

Manyalibo told her then how he had contrived to live his solitary life in the Forest. Those had been the days when he had learnt his skill as a hunter and had acquired his enormous knowledge.

"At last," he went on, "after those years when I had never spoken to another man or woman the Forest healed me. It took me back into itself again. And one day I came once more to my people."

The simplicity of that struck Thomasina almost with shock.

"But -" she said. "But were you welcomed? What did people say? What did they think?"

"They said nothing. I was there. In my place again."

"And the husband of the wife you - of that wife?"

"He had died for ever."

"And the wife? What had happened to her?"

"Her husband had beaten her, many times. She is Kondabate."

Kondabate, Thomasina thought with astonishment. And I had seen her always merely as Manyalibo's helpmeet, at my bed of sickness, in and round his hut, even sometimes still in his arms. And all along she had been once – she recalled hearing the term in sedate Salisbury on just one occasion – the other woman, the breaker of the accepted order.

It was not long after she had heard Manyalibo's story that Thomasina learnt that her notion of the order and permanence of the life of the village was in another way by no means in accord with reality.

She learnt it from Asofalinda.

She was sitting beside the girl watching her make a basket. Dreamily she admired her dexterity and, more, delighted once again in the way her weaving of supple stick against supple stick brought a regularity out of disordered conglomeration. Asofalinda looked up from her busy hands.

"This basket will be good when we go," she said.

"Go? Go where? What is this?"

"But in two days we go to the next place. The honey here is almost finished."

Thomasina realised that, despite having been told otherwise, she had somehow come to think of the village as being a permanency. As indeed it was. But it was permanent as itself only. As a place, there was nothing easier than to abandon its fragile mongongo-leaf huts and to make new ones elsewhere. She had known the honey season was near its end, but she had assumed that some other food would be garnered where they were from the Forest riches. The honey dances, which had taken place each evening during the season, would, she had idly thought, be replaced by some other form of dance intended to prepare the hunters to seek some other booty.

No, if the village life with its ritual dances, its agreed ways of doing things, its implicit order, was a permanency, it was also, with its ever-occurring changes in obedience to the random changes of the Forest, the very paradigm of the wind-blown, the temporary, the chancy.

That night, indeed, the last of the honey dances took place. The last, the longest and the best.

133

As darkness swiftly came on, more and more brightly combustible wood was piled on the fires in the centre of the circle of huts that constituted the village. Then the men gathered to one side of the darting high flames and the women to the other. Everywhere there was a susurration of expectancy, palpable as the heat from the fire.

Thomasina, sensing that on this occasion she could not without offence join either the women or the men – often as a creature from another world she had been seen as an honorary man – felt abruptly, as she had not done for weeks, that she was an outsider, an interloper.

But, almost at once with the beginning of the music all such thoughts were driven from her head. When she had first heard the music of the village it had meant nothing to her. It was, she felt then, only a series of plinkings and plonkings underlain with drumming that was, if anything, somewhat frightening. It had seemed as far from what she thought of as music, her own earnest renderings of Thalberg and Benedick, the roll and thunder of the great cathedral organ she had listened to every Sunday, as was the simple life of the village from the crowds and complexities of the London she had visited to make her preparations for Africa.

But, as night by night the honey season and its dances had gone by, the music made in the darkness of the surrounding Forest had slowly entwined itself into her. Now the plink-plink of the four-stringed harp-like instrument fashioned from a branch bent at just the right angle made together with that underbeat from the drums a music to her ears the full equal of Mendelssohn or Handel. It affected her in a quite different manner, but as powerfully, or even more so. The throbbing of the drums, at its strongest causing the very skin of her bosom to vibrate minutely in sympathy, could scatter from her mind all mundane thoughts. Worries were banished. Mosquito bites ceased to itch. The dampness of her clothes in the unending wet was forgotten. Her nagging anxiety about Fito, for whom she felt a particular concern still, and whether he was flirting with pretty Asofalinda too assiduously, simply went.

But more than the drums, more than the curiously affecting plink-plink of the harp, what had most moved her on the one night its voice had been added to the music had been an instrument she had never seen. Its sound had a quality of unearthliness that had seemed to lift her to another plane. In tone it was something like a bassoon, but of a deeper, more sonorous character. And it had been played, not from inside the circle of the village huts, but from somewhere out in the Forest beyond.

Its player, she knew, was Manyalibo. When the night before its notes had been added, tantalisingly briefly, to the other music she had looked for him to ask what it was and had seen he was no longer there. She had known then that this was something she ought not to inquire about, neither to Manyalibo nor to any of the other village men or women. That brief, mysterious music was a secret. True magic.

And now, on this last night of the honey dances, as the men on their side of the high-piled brightly-burning fire went in a long line jigging and jogging, acting as if they were in the Forest listening for the homing whine of the bees, singing a humming buzzing song, there suddenly broke in on the music once more that magical, sonorous booming that had sent through her such trembling of she knew not what.

At once she found the eerie, tears-bringing sound entering into her. She saw, too, that the dancers, unwavering in their dance, the men searching, the women flying tightly bunched, were as tied as she herself to that unearthly music coming from the darkness of the Forest. She had recognised in their eyes all during the day a yearning, a closed-in-ness that had been planted in them by the brief music of the night before. And now that hauntedness was being answered. The unearthly, mysterious sound, just a little reminiscent of the call of the kooloo apes she had once been privileged to hear, was entering into each and every one of them. It was the very voice of the Forest itself.

But now it was more than those few tantalising notes of the night before. Now it went on and on. It embraced them. It filled them.

At what moment it ended Thomasina was unable to tell. She had long before lost all sense of time under its spell. She was hardly aware of going to her hut, the sound of those booming sonorous notes no longer there. She was as unaware of flinging herself down on her bed of soft boughs. She fell simply into the deepest of sleeps.

Only next morning while the men and women of the village, seemingly determined to put into limbo those feelings of the night before, were busy with preparations for the move to whatever place next they were to settle, did she sit for a little and consider what the experience had meant to her. Then she wrote a few words in her memoranda book in an attempt to pin down what had happened, what her mind had undergone.

"*I have thought black*," she wrote eventually. "*Yes, I have truly at last thought black. I was at one with them all, thinking black. I was lost in feelings-thoughts. And, more, I know, thinking black is there in the mind of every soul on this earth. It is there waiting to be drawn up out of its own depths.*"

It was this self-discovery that, paradoxically, finally decided her in favour of civilisation as against the Forest in the combat that had been going on in her mind ever since under Manyalibo she had begun to feel the full fascination of the wholly African life. It had been a near thing. The night before, with that haunting, moving, mysterious music in her ears and flooding into her heart, she had had one brief moment of seeing herself as it were from the outside. And then she had looked at a person, a thirty-year-old spinster from Salisbury, Wiltshire, transported into a wholly different existence.

There am I, she had thought in that short moment of outside vision, a creature of the Forest. A Forest creature. I shall live like this for as long as I can see. I shall learn of the Forest, from the Forest. I will be of the Forest.

In the morning, partly perhaps from seeing the people of the village so sensibly bent about their humdrum tasks of gathering their possessions into bundles and binding them up, of carefully taking embers from the fire – the fire that the night before had flaringly illuminated a ritual of the very Forest itself - she found she had lost that conviction. She was back to finding her mind a battleground between those two altogether contrary aims, civilisation or savagedom.

Then, after she had set down in her memoranda book that thought about the universality of the potential to 'think black', she had laid the book down in her lap, lifted up her head and realised she had come to a decision. Or that a decision had come to her.

If thinking black was not necessarily something that could be done only when one was in and of the Forest, then she could safely continue with her quest. She could find the healing plant that had so ironically escaped from Doctor Diver's hands at the very moment of proving its efficacy against the typhoid fever. She could take it back to England. She would one day witness its use throughout society in combating that dread, raging plague.

She rose up from the bundled-stick chair that could happily be left behind where the village had been to decay and rot and join the black underlay of the Forest, and she prepared to set out with her friends for wherever it would be that they would settle again.

But she would not be with them for long, she knew.

CHAPTER 12

The currents of the two streams were sharply different in colour. The main stream, large enough to be called a river, was of the same milky-tea brown as the mighty river Zaire itself. Its tributary, by some geological freak, flowed into it as a long swirl of brick-red.

"Blood red," Tom said, standing stretching limbs cramped from hours of journeying along the bumpy winding track.

She turned to David, yawning hippo-like beside her.

"You realise what that means?" she asked.

"That you've got an over-active imagination?"

She grinned.

"Well, okay," she said, "though in point of the fact the imagination is the natives' more than a hundred years ago."

"Eh?"

"Come on. What did the people of the village call the second place that Thomasina stayed with them?"

"Oh, yes. Yes. Forget the gobbledegook word, but it meant the place of blood, didn't - hey, you mean this is it? It? Where she actually was?"

"Well, it's hardly likely there are two streams doing what these two do anywhere else. Certainly not within a hundred miles of this area."

"You must be right. So, this is it, eh? The actual spot where dear old Thomasina set off on the last part of her journey."

"And from where we're going to set off, into what you're pleased to call the primeval jungle, just on the other side of the river there. Always provided it turns out that bloody Tim Lunn has just gone for a bit of a walk rather than having disappeared for ever."

***

As soon as the long laden straggle of the village people reached the riverside clearing where it had been decided, by mysterious common intent, they should settle I recognised the place. It was unmistakable. Doctor Diver's notes had described it precisely. Into the wide slow-flowing stream, its waters just the shade of those of the mighty Congo, there shot a long feather of bright red from its smaller tributary.

The moment I saw that swirl of red water I felt it was an omen, an omen confirming my decision of two days before to resume my delayed search for Doctor Diver's plant. To do so, I would have to get across to the far side of the tea-brown river, the colour that reminded me, paddling up the Congo long ago of tea in the evening back at home in the Close. The crossing would present considerable difficulties. But they could be overcome. They must be overcome.

I will need all the help I can persuade Manyalibo to give me. I will need, on the far side of the river, the services once again of young Fito, and perhaps other bearers. Nor would my journey there be easy. Doctor Diver's notes had said that the Forest across the river was more difficult to traverse than anywhere he had met with earlier. He had written of much swampland, of fearful plagues of insects, spiders, driver ants, of infestation of the deadly ompenle snake.

But the end of my long quest is within sight. I will not let any obstacles now, however awesome, deflect me from it.

***

Major Yombton-Smith, legs apart in the at-ease position in his jungle greens, beat at his right calf with the stick cut from the Forest which he carried in place of a swagger-cane.

"By golly," he said, "I'm going to give your Mr Lunn one hell of a rocket when he does turn up."

Tom did her best to flutter eyelashes that were too stubby to make much play with.

"Oh, Jacky," she said, "don't be too fierce with him. We do need him, you know. I mean, he's the one who knows where the rest of Thomasina's diaries are hidden."

"Yes. See you're right, actually. Have to box a bit clever at this stage of the game. But all the same the fellow's a confounded nuisance."

"There I agree," David who had been visibly fretting, broke in. "you did tell him Major, didn't you, that there's quite a hefty fee attached to this?"

"Oh, I briefed him all right. But trouble with types like that is they don't really want money. Prefer the free and easy life. Can't say I altogether blame him for that, actually."

"That's all very well. But, damn it all, the whole of this business depends on the fellow. Months of organisation. Arrangements across half the world. Never mind how much of Far Flung Film's capital's involved. We can't have it all go to waste just because this character prefers your free and easy life."

Tom giggled.

"Oh, Teigh, don't be so pompous. What's got into you?"

"I'm not being pompous," David snapped. "It's just that a heck of a lot of time and trouble's been invested in this, and I'm damned if I'll see it go under just because some wildcat prospector takes it into his head to go walkabout."

Tom could hardly contain her laughter.

"Honestly, Teigh. If you could hear yourself. Calm down, for heaven's sake. Things like this are all part of the game."

"That's where you're bloody wrong. This is not a game set up for your amusement. There's a hell of a lot at stake, and -"

"I say, look here..."

Major Yombton-Smith beat a yet more ferocious tattoo on his unoffending calf.

"Listen, you chaps, this is what I think we'd better do. We'll give Mr Lunn just twenty-four hours, and if he hasn't reported by that time I'll organise a recce. Dig him out."

Without waiting for any agreement, he turned on his heel and strode off to the big, dilapidated, mud-walled house that had once been the centre of camp Alcott.

"Now you've upset him," Tom said to David. "All that unseemly rowing."

"Who was rowing?"

"Oh, well, yes, I suppose I was as bad as you. Worse. I quite like a row."

"Don't I know it, you sodding hooligan. But I suppose I was being a bit pompous. It's just that whatever your Major Jacky says gets up my nose. I mean that manuscript of his – what a joke! I bet his bloody recce doesn't succeed in locating old Tom Gunn."

"Oh, I don't know. Say what you like about poor Jacky, he is efficient. Look at the way he's planned things. Every T dotted, every I crossed. Or whichever it is."

"Well, I suppose you're right actually. I don't know that I exactly admire it, but he does get things done. Your military mind, applying set rules to every situation. And as long as you've got enough of them, it does seem to work."

"Except they didn't stop Tom Gunn wandering off against orders."

Tom giggled again.

***

When Jacky Yombton-Smith's twenty-four hours had gone by without any sign of Tim Lunn re-appearing he at once launched into his well-prepared 'recce'. The rubber dinghy he had had ready to ferry his Filmforce across the river was put into service to take parties of bearers – 'hunter group' – to the far side where they were paraded at the Forest edge in squarely neat, if patently puzzled, clumps.

Tom and David, forbidden to join the search on the grounds of inexperience in 'Forest discipline', a fiat also applied to Reg Blandy and Josh Perkins, watched the performance from under the shade of the hundreds of umbrella-like leaves of a parasol tree. They did not quite know whether to be amused or impressed.

Reg, however, had no doubts. As the Major despatched the groups one by one into the great hanging curtain of green in front of them, he gave a little bracing jerk to his shoulders under his khaki bush-shirt.

"There's a chap who knows how to go about things," he said. "Did you see how he numbered off his search squads just now? It won't be long before he locates this Mr Lunn. Mark my words."

"Care to place a small bet?" David asked. "Quid for every hour either side of, say midday?"

"The currency here is the Zaire," Reg Blandy said. "The same name as the country is called now. And I'm not a betting man."

Naughtily David looked all round at the looming walls of the Forest.

"You know," he said, "I wouldn't have thought the currency just here is the Zaire. It's more like the human head, if you ask me. This is the primeval jungle, after all."

"Shut up, Teigh," Tom said. "When we actually get into the jungle you may not find it so much of a joke."

"In any case," Reg said, "I'm going off to check over my cameras. You don't want to find I can't shoot when we get going this afternoon."

Josh, who had been standing beside Reg in his customary far away daze, suddenly came to life.

"Yes," he said. "Yes."

"Yes what, Josh dear?" Tom asked.

"Um? Er - yes. I think I ought to collect my mic and see if I can't pick up some Forest wild-track while there's no one else about."

"Here, Josh?"

"Well, yes, thought I'd go up along that stream with the reddish water. I wouldn't think the Forest would sound much different this side of the big stream or the other. Would you?"

"No. No, I don't mean that. I imagine the sounds for five hundred miles in any direction would be just the same. No, what I meant was: are you sure you ought to go wandering into what David will call the primeval jungle all on your own?"

"Oh, I should think I'd be all right. I worked on a film in Borneo once. Rainforest's okay if you just keep your wits about you."

Tom looked at him.

"And you do that, Josh dear?"

"Oh, well, yes. Yes, I do. Well, keep my ears open, and it comes to the same thing, you know."

"Then good luck."

"And don't be too long," David added. "Remember, Major Smith-Yombton's going to come back in an hour or so dragging poor Tim Lunn behind him. Or so Reg says."

"It's Yombton-Smith actually," Josh replied.

He wandered off towards the mud hut in the circle surrounding the main house which had been allocated to him.

"There you go," David sighed. "So what do we two do now, left all on our ownio? Ah, I know. We take advantage of Major Jacky's back being turned, we sneak off both together to my hut and we -"

"No, we do not."

"But why not, for heaven's sake? I mean, what else is there to do?"

"We could check over our kit, be ready to go as soon as Jacky gets back. Or we could discuss what we need to get on film."

"Oh, sod that. My idea's a million times better. And your Jacky's not going to find Tom Gunn for hours. If he ever does."

"In which case, sweetheart, we'll be in the shit. You most of all. B-J's never going to keep you on his payroll if this is a total disaster."

"But – but - hey, no, you're joking. You must be. You pig."

"Well, I was. But I've begun to think about it. You know, if Tim Lunn really never does turn up, this whole thing is actually bound to abort. Thomasina's diary doesn't say enough to lead us exactly to wherever she hid the rest of it. So there'll be no film."

"God, yes, I suppose you're right. Christ, you know, it was a hell of a gamble diving off into the primev - diving off into Africa on the chance of meeting up with old Tom Gunn."

"Gamble, yes. Grant you that. But it was a gamble you were just as keen to take as I was. Or to con B-J into taking. And it wasn't actually all that much of a risk. From all we'd heard of Tom Gunn - no, fucked if I'll call him that. From all we'd heard of Tim Lunn he's someone who is caught sight of frequently enough. I mean, Major, Jacky got hold of him quite easily in the first place."

"Okay. But how hot are you at praying?"

"Not a lot, as you very well know. But I am pretty good at waiting for something to turn up. A real little Mr Whatshisname. In Dickens, isn't it? One I had to read at school."

"Micawber, you ignorant slob. But, listen, do you really think B-J'll cut me loose if this bites the dust? Jesus, I'd never even thought about it."

"No, you wouldn't, would you? Popping in and out of jobs all your life. But you may not find that so easy now. Times is hard, me boy."

"You don't have to tell me that. God, what will I do?"

"Live off me, I suppose. Till times ain't so hard. If ever."

"But - well, I couldn't do that."

"Hark at him. Couldn't possibly live off a woman."

"Oh, okay... I know it's silly in a way, but that was my instinctive reaction. Of course, I could live off you. For a bit. Share your lettuce, if I thought I was going to get another job in a month or two. But I wouldn't get one, necessarily, not nowadays."

"So what? If we were a married couple and you happened to be made redundant or something, we wouldn't split up on the strength of that, would we?"

"Well, no. No. But that's different."

"Oh, yes? Why different?"

"I don't know. It just is. I mean, we'd be committed then, wouldn't we?"

"And we're not committed now? After three years together? And with you saying *come into my hut* every five minutes?"

"But that's just sex."

"And our commitment's been just sex all along? Is that what you're saying? It's been radically different from Do *you, David, take Teresa Olivia to be your wedded wife*?"

David nodded his rugged, wide face to and fro, working it out.

"No, of course it's not different," he said. "But... but, well, it is. Somehow. I mean, don't you really think so, too? In your heart of hearts?"

Now it was Tom's turn to be perplexed.

"God knows," she said at last. "I mean, I'd have said it isn't different, not different at all, if I'd been asked in the ordinary way, back home, discussing it with friends or something. But - oh, I don't know. Here. It sort of seems to be another question altogether. God knows why. But it just does."

"The baleful influence of the great primeval J?"

Tom frowned in quick irritation.

"No. No, it isn't - well, I suppose it might be, in a way. I suppose it's

144

something to do with the isolation anyhow. Being all on our own here. I feel sort of challenged."

"All on our own with little Reg ever at your elbow? And dear old Josh full of happy chatter?"

"Oh, don't be silly. You know we are on our own. And Major Jacky doesn't make a ha'p'orth of difference either."

"Well, he did put us into separate huts. And that makes a difference, at least to me."

"No, stop it. When we're having a serious conversation for once."

"Yes. Sorry. I got you off the point."

"If I really knew what the point was..."

"But it is, what?"

"Well, just that here, here, I do somehow sort of believe in marriage. That it's different. When you solemnly swear to everything."

"But Christ... Christ. I mean, no, I'm – I'm not ready, if that's what you're suggesting. Sorry. Sorry. I sort of thought I was, but I'm not. And, well, there it is."

Tom burst out into laughter.

The sound of it clattered away across the tea-brown water of the wide stream.

CHAPTER 13

Josh Perkins brought Tim Lunn into camp Alcott. It was late in the afternoon. Major Yombton-Smith's hunter group on the far side of the river had not yet returned. David and Tom were in the hut that had been allocated to Tom.

When they heard Josh plaintively calling, "er - anyone about?" they emerged. After a couple of minutes.

They saw a man of sixty or even seventy, with a mop of grey tousled hair, a drooping grey raggedy moustache and eyes of a very pale blue, frequently blinking. His shirt and trousers, somewhat torn, were of a khaki so faded that it was little removed from yellow-whiteness. On the back of his head was a sola topee of the same aeons-bleached shade.

They had known at once whom he must be.

"Mr Lunn? Tim Lunn?" Tom said, marching up with her hand held out. "I'm Tom Mountjoy. This is David Teigh. We're delighted to meet you."

"Oh. Ah."

The aged prospector seemed at a loss for any further form of communication.

"Where... where did Josh find you?" David asked, with excessive heartiness. "He has told you who he is, hasn't he? Josh Perkins, our sound man"

"Hm. Yes. Yes, think so. Not sure... not sure what a sound man is. You're... you're this film lot, are you? Somebody said something about you. I think."

With painful patience Tom explained.

Tim Lunn shook his head.

"Yes. But I don't know about all that. You see, I've got my work.

There's uranium somewhere in the Forest, you know. Uranium."

He extended a long arm with a gnarled pointing forefinger and swept it in a wide arc that embraced the whole greenly brooding Forest round. He could have been the very picture of some hermit, or of Robinson Crusoe himself.

"And you hope to find it someday, this uranium?" David said, over-helpfully.

He received an angry glare from the pale blue eyes.

"Hope? Hope? There's no question of hope. I will find it. I will. Look at the colour of the water in the stream there. Red. Red. Does that mean nothing to you?"

"Well, yes, as a matter of fact it does," David said. "It means quite a lot to us. You see, Thomasina le Mesurier in her diaries absolutely identifies this spot. Er - because of that red water running into the river here like – well, like a jet of blood. The Place of Blood. That, apparently, was how this actual spot was called by the natives she was with."

The old man shook his head with weary indifference.

"I don't know anything about that," he said. "Don't know what you're talking about. What the colour of that stream means is that the earth where it rises is red-coloured too. And that's one of my best chances for uranium deposits. They may be anywhere, though. Anywhere. Take my word for it."

David was about to leap in to bring the subject back to the diaries. But Tom forestalled him.

"Mr Lunn," she said, "I have a feeling that we can work together now for both our benefits. We are anxious, as I said, to find the rest of Thomasina le Mesurier's diaries, and, since you must have come across them while you were searching for signs of uranium, I imagine you would be interested in returning to that area. To make a wider sweep, or whatever. So what if we combine forces? I'm sure you could find uses for all the porters we've got."

Tim Lunn did not answer. His pale blue eyes were blinking even more rapidly.

"You don't - you do remember where you found the diaries?" Tom asked in sudden panic.

The old man swallowed.

"Diaries," he said. "Yes. Yes, diaries."

"You remember finding them?"

"Of course I remember. You don't think I'm gaga, do you? I suppose you've decided the uranium deposits here are just an old man's hallucination. Have you? Have you?"

"No, no. I promise... I dare say, in fact, you have a better chance of finding uranium than we have of – er - finding those diaries."

"Hm," Tim Lunn barked with continuing aggression. "There's no difficulty about the diaries. They're in a cairn. I suppose you'd call it a cairn. Thought it was just a termite mound when I saw it first. But I noticed it was made of stones and not that mud termites make with their saliva. So I had the curiosity – I'm a man of great curiosity, you know – I had the curiosity to investigate."

"And you found the diaries," Tom said encouragingly, "and you took away a few specimens?"

Tim Lunn looked abruptly affronted.

"And why wouldn't I? Are you saying I'm a thief? They were left there, going begging. And they might have been worth a few pounds. They were. So why shouldn't I have sold them? I have my expenses, you know. I have my expenses."

"And it's just those that we'd like to help you with," David put in quickly. "We're certainly prepared - I don't know if Major Yombton-Smith made this clear, but we're certainly prepared to pay a substantial fee for your help. A very substantial fee."

"You think I'm a beggar? You think I'm in need of a hand-out? I assure you, young man, I shall die a millionaire. A multi-millionaire."

"Yes, yes, of course," Tom said. "But in the meanwhile can you use our assistance? Major Yombton-Smith is organising our expedition, and you can be sure it will go like clockwork. So won't you come with us?"

The old prospector glared at her for a few seconds. Then he answered.

"Oh, very well, since you're so insistent."

*

Tom had more than a little difficulty in preventing Jacky Yombton-Smith, when he arrived back as darkness was falling, plainly bone-tired and in an ill temper, from giving Tim Lunn the 'rocket' he had threatened to deliver earlier. But, making herself a good deal more girlish than David had ever seen her, she contrived at last to cajole him out of it.

All during the following day when preparations for going into the Forest proper were in hand she had to nursemaid the old prospector. Half the time she was heading him off from setting out on his own again, and the other half she was doing her best to prevent him further upsetting Major Yombton-Smith.

When the Major was conducting a foot inspection of his team of porters, making each man show him one by one the calloused soles of his naked feet just as if he was counting the metal studs in the boots of his company in England before cross-country manoeuvres, the old prospector stationed himself well within voice range and fired off loud comments.

"What's the fellow doing now? What does he want with all those paddlers anyhow? None of them knows a thing about the Forest, easy to see that."

"Well, you know, Mr Lunn," Tom was constrained to reply sotto voce, "Major Yombton-Smith has led a good many expeditions in his time."

"Expeditions? Expeditions? You don't want expeditions in the Forest. You want to go there and keep your eyes open. That's all. Just go there. Be there."

"Yes, I'm sure, but –"

"And what's he want with all the stuff he's expecting them to carry? Eh? Eh? You have to travel light in the Forest. Only way to cover the ground. That's what people don't understand. You're never going to make a really big hit unless you cover the ground. But I shall. Yes, I shall. One day I'll make the big hit. See if I don't. One day."

"Yes, tell me about that. Let's go over there where there's some shade under that tree..."

For half an hour then she managed to keep apart the two men she felt she could not do without. But then the ancient prospector evaded her again and got himself to where Jacky Yombton-Smith was busy dividing his porters' loads into meticulously equal piles.

"What's he got there?" he demanded, peering at the nearest heap as Tom came hurrying up. "Tins? Tins of fruit? What's he want with tins of fruit? And what's this? What's this?"

Before Tom could prevent him he had seized a can from the next-door pile and was holding it up reading the label.

"Spaghetti," he screeched, breaking into a choppy peal of laughter. "Spaghetti. He's taking spaghetti into the Forest."

Major Jacky came striding up.

"Excuse me, Lunn," he said, barely concealing his fury, "but I would be obliged if you would put that back exactly where you found it. It'll be a confounded nuisance if we're wanting tinned fruit one night and we find we're landed with spaghetti."

Tom managed to slide the offending can out of Tim Lunn's grasp and replaced it in its correct pile.

"Sorry about that, Jacky."

She contrived once again to lead the prospector off, leaving Major Jacky arranging his neat stacks of fruit cans, spaghetti tins, rice bags and sardines together with medicine supplies laid out in patterned rows on plastic sheets, the vitamin tablets, the sun creams, the antiseptic ointments, the boxes of plasters, the packets of bandages (in order of increasing widths), the insect repellent sprays, the malaria pills, the water-purifying tablets, the aspirins, the antibiotics with their sealed syringes beside them, the anti-histamine creams, the anti-diarrhoea medicines, the differently coloured packets of anti-dysentery tablets.

When they took a break for lunch, at precisely 1300 hours – old N'goi was not only a competent cook but could produce his meals exactly when required – Tim Lunn refused to join the common table. So Tom spent the whole time nervously looking over her shoulder to where her charge had chosen to sit.

"He'll softly and suddenly vanish away," David whispered to her, increasing her vexation.

There were Major Jacky's counter-complaints to placate.

"I mean, my fellows made valiant efforts all yesterday to find the chap, and then he turns up here bold as brass and with never a word of explanation, much less apology."

"Yes, I know, Jacky dear. But he's sort of a law to himself, I'm afraid. We'll just have to put up with it."

"I dare say, old girl. But it'll be devilish awkward when we march in the Forest."

"Well, we'll try to keep him out of your hair as much as we can. But we do have to have him, you know. He's the only one who's seen the cairn where those diaries are hidden. And that's what this is all about."

"Yes, I appreciate that. But you'll find he'll let us down in the end. That type always does. Can't you just get a good bearing out of him, and pay the old bugger off? Excuse my French."

"No go. He doesn't do anything much by bearings, apparently just relies on remembering his way about the Forest. And I suppose he does that all right, I gather he's been wandering through it for twenty years if not more."

"Well, all right. I suppose at this stage of the game all we can do is just carry on regardless."

"Yes. Carry on it is. Regardless, as you say."

***

Thomasina eventually left on the last stage of her quest with young Fito as her only companion. She had thought of asking Manyalibo to accompany her. But at once she had seen that his life now was too deeply woven into that of the village.

In any case, she had calculated, Fito on his own should be enough. The swamp patch under the waterfall split by the yellow-fanged rock where Doctor Diver's plants grew was, according to his notes, only a week's walking away. She should be back at the village at the Place of Blood in fourteen days then. Or at most fifteen or sixteen. Then, carried in triumph on Fito's head, there would be her biggest Wardian case with, still alive and growing in its steamy confinement, as many specimens of the saviour plant as she could fit in.

After that she might indeed need more bearers. They would see her safely on the first part of her journey back, to the great Congo River. From there she would go with difficulty perhaps, but not insuperably so, to the sea, to England, to the vindication of the memory of Doctor Diver.

For the first two days of her journey through the Forest it seemed that Fito's sole presence was going to be all indeed that she needed. She was so much better acquainted with the ways of the Forest than she had been before that she was able to make much faster progress than in her early days. With Fito following, the precious Wardian case on his head and not much else, she was able to put behind her in the course of eight or nine hours' walking almost twice as many miles as she had done when M'bene and Snail-Shell had also been of her party, burdened with all the things she had then thought indispensable. Wryly she recalled the days when she had depended on Chollet's preserved vegetables brought all the way from London on the advice of Mr Galton's book.

In the cool gloom now, the gloom she had come to feel as being almost the only proper surroundings for life to be lived in, she made her way steadily forward. Without thought, she chose the best path, avoiding obstacles with all the unreflecting ease with which she might have once stepped round some horse droppings in a Salisbury street.

From time to time she drew in a deep, pleasing breath of the musty air. Almost unconsciously she picked out from it the various odours Manyalibo had taught her to recognise. From the smell of the first tentative drops of urine from some sportive monkey hidden in the high foliage above she took warning and avoided its malicious intentions for both Fito and herself. When she detected bats' urine she gave Fito a quick word to ask if he cared to halt and climb the tree it came from. Bats tasted like the quail she had once eaten as a great treat in the little house in the Close, though gamier. On food of this sort the two of them could easily subsist, friends of the all-embracing

Forest.

***

"Blow winds and crack your cheeks," David said. "Rage, blow, you cataracts and hurricanoes. Spout till you have drenched our steeples, drowned the cocks. You sulphurous and thought-executing fires, vaunt-couriers to oak-cleaving thunderbolts, singe my white - no, black, blackish, going on grey - my black head. And thou, all-shaking thunder, strike flat the thick rotundity of the world."

Tom looked at him.

"What the hell's all that about? It must be poetry."

"Jesus. It must be poetry. It's Shakespeare. It's King Lear. You dumb, ignorant savage."

"Okay, okay. You know I've never read any more Shakespeare than I was made to at school."

David shook his head wearily.

"God," he said, "I sometimes wonder how I put up with you. You're even more ignorant than an ignorant savage. Really you are."

"One," Tom said, "savages aren't ignorant, or they're only ignorant of things that can't possibly concern them. Think of Thomasina's Manyalibo. And, two, you put up with me, and I put up with you, because it so happens we're compatible. Or ninety percent compatible."

"Well, yes. Yes. I know that. I know both things. Savages, yes. Some very knowledgeable, others dumb like anywhere else. Compatible, yes, yes. Terrifically."

"Then why all the spout and blow. For once there's no sign of any whatsits - hurricanoes."

David sighed.

"Just really psyching myself up for the Forest tomorrow," he said. "The plunge into chaos and old night. All that. Think I'm going to enjoy it. Revel, you might say. I think."

CHAPTER 14

The first two days of Thomasina's final march proved to be the only time when the Forest was kind to her. Within an hour of starting out on the third day she and Fito encountered a tract which, it seemed, had been taken over entirely by colony after colony of huge yellow-and-black spiders. They were a sort Thomasina had never in all her Forest rambling with Manyalibo come across. She had seen nothing even like them.

Each was almost as big in its bulbous body, to Thomasina's eyes, as the egg of a sparrow seen neatly in its nest in the orderly Wiltshire countryside. Their webs, which often stretched curtain-like for as much as three feet across, were not the silvery-grey of familiar English spiders but a violent yellow, the same virulent yellow as the splotches on their bodies. When at last she nerved herself up to push her way through one, past which she could see no easy way, she found it so strong that it offered a palpable resistance. It was, she felt, as if she had had to break through a veil of fine cambric. Only there was nothing pleasing in its clinging texture.

But that was not the only difficulty the creatures presented. Fito, who equally had never seen anything in any way like these giants, announced they were bad juju. They should turn back, he said.

For a while Thomasina taunted him with lack of courage. But no amount of scorn could persuade him to go on. At last she decided the only thing to do was to set him an example, and she marched off by herself, deliberately pushing through every wide-stretched web she came across.

To her relief, when she had gone in this manner some fifty yards or so, she heard behind her a plaintive cry and realised that Fito was following. But her success had not come before she had found herself covered from the collar of her blouse to the hem of her skirt in a thick layer of the criss-crossing foul yellow strands.

And then she was bitten.

She had taken care whenever she had noticed one of the yellow-blotched creatures running with horrible swiftness along the strands of its web to dodge to the side. But now she had failed to see one of them. It must have been brushed off from its web on to the lower part of her skirt. From there it had run in a moment up on to her blouse, black legs scurrying so rapidly as almost to merge into one another. Before she could make any move to flick it off it reached her exposed neck. And then she felt a jab of pain so intense it made her cry out aloud.

Fito, behind her, stopped in his tracks.

"The Forest is not kind," he pronounced, with an edge of fear in his voice. "You will die a little. Perhaps you will die completely."

Thomasina, the piercing pain of the bite hardly slackening stood in an almost equal state of consternation. She felt a trickle of blood running down into the collar of her blouse. She seemed powerless even to raise her hand and try to halt the flow.

The spider, she saw from her state of transfixed stupor, was darting, scrambling down her other sleeve. It dropped off on to the black squelchy ground at her feet.

Then – it could not have been in actuality more than half a minute later – she began to come to her senses. The pain of the bite, she realised, had grown less. Nor was she feeling any other symptoms. Nothing of what she had feared in a rush of panic had materialised. No paralysis, no fits, none of half a dozen other half-envisaged calamities.

She brushed the blood from her neck, and noted that the pain now had considerably abated. Cautiously exploring, she found the wound, deep though it had seemed, had already closed.

She turned to Fito.

"Look," she said, "it is nothing. I am well. The Forest is our friend still."

Fito, plainly, was not wholly convinced. But when Thomasina began pushing onwards once more through the thick, clinging yellow veils he followed.

She was bitten again, once, before that extraordinary nightmare stage of her journey was over. But, encouraged by the outcome of her earlier experience, she managed on that occasion not even to cry out, though again the pain of the bite – it was on her forearm where her sleeve had got pushed up without her realising – was like being pierced by a needle straight from the flame.

They spent some time after emerging from the spiders' territory in resting, and after that made good progress again for a little. But, when there were still two hours of daylight remaining, they found themselves faced with going of the most discouraging sort.

Ahead, as far as they could see in either direction, there rose, not the usual immense trees leaving the Forest floor comparatively clear, but a thick-growing wilderness. What must have happened only a few months earlier, Thomasina realised, was that a tornado had caused more havoc than usual among the Forest giants. Where a single mighty tree might have fallen – as she remembered happening all too vividly – here perhaps as many as twenty seemed to have come crashing down all at the same time.

Then what had happened had been what always occurred after a tree fall had made a sudden clearing in the Forest. The light pouring in from above where the thick-layered leaf canopy had abruptly disappeared would start a frenzy of new growth down at the level of the Forest floor. In the stretch ahead of her now that frenzy had been multiplied twentyfold.

A no-holds-barred rush to the light had begun. Self for self, she thought. It is that and no more. The devil take the hindmost. It is a disregard for order and decency as if it were a mob in some city riot. A heartless jostling and trampling. The weakest to the wall.

Seeds, lying long dormant in the cool of the Forest floor, struck suddenly by the full heat of the blazing equatorial sun had burst into life. Into growth. Reaching and reaching for the sky, for that sunlight to bask in their lives long. Almost visibly growing in the fetid warmth, spindly shoots and saplings, close-packed, had pushed and struggled against each other, climbing, climbing to the light. To where at last they could spread branches and leaves to the sun, and leave their competitors, only a few feet or a few inches below them, to wither in the renewed gloom and die.

But the effect of this mass struggle had been to make the Forest facing her now into a thicket of close-packed tree poles. To pass through the area they covered appeared almost an impossibility. An hour's work in the entwined mass might get the two of them no further than a hundred yards forward, even fifty.

"We will have to rest here," she said to Fito.

"Yes, yes, I will make fire."

I write for a few minutes before we attempt to find our way round, or force our way through the terrible matted tangle that lies in our path. I should be filled with new resolution. But my night was so afflicted with dreams, no, by one nightmare of appalling vividness, that I find myself prey to a dragging unwillingness to set one foot in front of another. I do not know why I should have been so enmired as I slept. Was it the effect of the spider bites I had received? They seemed to have left me unharmed, but perhaps some venom had entered my blood to rampage in my veins. Certainly I cannot put down my trouble to lack of comfort. Dear Fito had made us a fire and a half and the pliant branches he had found for my bed were all that they could have been. And, no, I cannot blame indigestion. Our meal of agouma cake, that sustaining stuff made from the oil of wild mango seeds, gave me not a pang. But such dreams I had. One above all remains at the forefront of my mind. I was at the place where poor M'bene was killed. What I saw in my dream at the start was, to the best of my recollection, what I had seen then. I was lying, as I had lain, on the side of the gully. The very tints of the leaves of the plants close to my face, as I had seen them in the flashes of lightning during that terrible tornado, were as they had been. The exact pattern of the bark on the tree some few yards away was as it had been impressed on my mind. The leopard was crouching as I had seen it crouch on that dreadful day, surely the worst I have yet endured. Its thick tail was thumping and thumping in anger on the ground behind it. But from thenceforward dream and reality parted company, horribly. I found I had in my hand the revolver which had, in fact, remained in its waterproof wrappings for my entire sojourn in the Forest until after M'bene's death I disposed of it. With it in my dream I shot the leopard. Would that this had at least been no dream and that my impetuous M'bene was with me yet. But that was not to be, except within this dream of mine. And there the result of my willingness to shoot was very much otherwise than it would have been in reality. The eyes of the beast in front of me glazed in death, true. Its claws still dug into the ground not six feet from my face. Its threshing tail stilled in the very act of beating the sodden earth under it. But in seconds an enormous hole appeared in that blunt cat face. Blood poured from it in a stream. Nor was it red blood. It became in moments a river of thick, viscous, sinuously spreading green. Slowly it advanced towards me. I was now, somehow, at a distance from the leopard corpse, from the wide source of that vile river. But nearer and nearer the virid jelly-like stream approached. At last it touched me. Coldly. With a horrible chilliness. And I awoke. Fito's fire was a glowing heap of embers, still giving out generous heat. But some heavy drop from the ever-dripping moisture of the Forest had fallen on my face. Nothing more than that. I wiped it away. But I could not wipe away the impression of that dream. I lay for long awake. I may have slept again a little before dawn. But the grip of that nightmare is at my throat still.

***

They were making good progress through the Forest, Major Jacky in the lead slapping at his green-trousered thigh with his length of whippy stick at every stride. Behind him came the long file of porters. On their heads, carried with nonchalant ease, were their carefully calculated 70lb loads, the boxes of food cans, the medical supplies, the rolled hammocks, the Millbank water-filter bags, the folding tables, the folding chairs – "Chairs, chairs," old Tim Lunn had exclaimed as they had set out, "are we going to sit about like old ladies at a tea-party?" – Reg's second camera, his cans and cans of film stock, the steel box containing money for 'dash', the canvas-encased rifles and shotguns, the stoves, their jerry cans of fuel, Major Jacky's pet radio transceiver, the formidable chests of tools, saws, hammers, axes, and the neat coils of various thicknesses of rope.

David had whispered to Tom when he had first seen those.

"Hey. What d'you think Thomasina's famous Many-alibis would

have made of those? Not exactly his one Forest creeper for each particular use."

But Tom had frowned.

"Stop knocking the poor chap. Jacky knows what he's doing, down to the last pot of Vaseline to stop ants climbing the hammock strings."

"Oh, yes, that was very clever. But all the same..."

Behind the porters Reg and Josh came, again in single file. Reg had his light camera on his shoulder and every now and again dipped out of the line and buzzed away at some particularly dramatic clump of tumbling fern or at the underside of some garish fungus. Josh, recording satchel on his back, equally pointed his dark grey sausage microphone up towards the leaf canopy above from which had issued the mysterious cry of a bird or the wild whooping of a monkey troop. Just behind them old N'goi loped along, his pink vest slipping easily and somehow contentedly through the green gloom.

And, some twenty yards to the rear, Tim Lunn followed. He seemed to be pretending that the long line of porters ahead was not in fact there. But he nevertheless matched Major Jacky's pace stride for stride.

Ahead the great trees and the huge swinging bundles of liana were a formless haze of green laced with the faintly phosphorescent white of the tree-trunks. Behind, the same indeterminate greenishness closed in on them again like the deep still waters of a lake.

"Jesus," David suddenly broke out. "It's cold. It's bloody cold."

Tom half turned to him as she tramped along.

"For God's sake, Teigh," she said. "What did you expect? You've read Thomasina's diaries. Of course it's cold when the sun's cut off like this. Well, cool. It's cool. Thomasina mentions it time and time again."

"Oh, I know. But this is it. It's happening to *me*. And I'll tell you something. I don't bloody like it. I don't like any of it. Not the cold – okay, the cool, then – not all this damn sprawling, creeping, intruding vegetation, not the damn disorder of it, not the stinking smell of it, not the whole appalling mess and muddle of – Christ, what was that?"

From somewhere above a bird had uttered a single high screeching note.

"It's a bird," Tom said, without much sympathy. "For fuck's sake, Teigh, take a hold of yourself."

David's eyes flashed with undirected rage.

"That's not a bird," he snapped. "It's not a bird-song. It's a sodding scream of pain, that's what it is. A scream of pain."

Tom made no reply.

For a quarter of an hour or more they tramped on in silence, past the huge whitish trunks of the trees towering up to the leaf canopy two hundred feet away, past the long trails of liana dangling from them, past the banks of huge ferns, the sprouting unnatural growths of fungi.

Then Tom took up the intermittent conversation they had been having before David's outburst.

"You know," she said, "just where we're walking now may very well be that area of the Forest Thomasina had so much difficulty getting through, where a tornado had brought down so many big trees and the secondary growth shooting up in their place had created such an obstacle. That tree there and the one just ahead with that creeper round it in those extraordinary regular rings; they may be a couple of the actual saplings she saw, the ones that triumphed in the race to the sun. They must be at least a hundred years old to have got to that size now."

But David did not respond.

***

It had taken Thomasina and Fito every bit as long as she had feared to fight their way through the area of storm damage when they had decided there was no easy way round. Fito hacked and hacked with his machete at the saplings and seedlings ranged like bars in front of them in their fantastic climb to the sunlight. Several times they had had to make their way round the huge trunk of a fallen tree at the cost of a whole hour's toil, pushing and squirming along its unending girth, as tall as the Wiltshire cottages Thomasina had walked past on her rambles with Doctor Diver, rounding at last its uptorn buttresses with the roots that had been under them dangling like a frizz of disordered hair. Once they had climbed over one of these fallen titans, in the vain hope that this was a speedier way of making progress.

Oh yes, Thomasina had thought as at last she had slid to the ground on its far side, scratched and sweat-bathed. Oh yes, no doubt Mr Darwin was right and even this monster we have just toiled over came to be as it was because it grew from a seed, fruit of its ancestors' painful discovery of a way to preserve it. The iron-hard seed-shell developed over so many generations – Manyalibo had shown her how they could be split in two to make useful vessels – was a proof of that. But how I wish Mr Darwin had made an enormous error and that, when such a monster tree as this thought of securing its progenies' future, it had not embarked on such an effective way of clearing the Forest round.

But, true enough, all the wild fury of growth, the tangled extravaganza, was no doubt the manifestation of a greater, over-riding order.

Yet would it had never come to be.

However, emerge from it all at last they did. They were rewarded then with one day of easy journeying. The ground ahead was sloping gently downwards. Walking, where the huge trees were widely spaced in their vast columns, was pleasantly unimpeded. Thomasina felt a growing elation with every step.

Doctor Diver's notes on the stage of his expedition that had brought him, incidentally as he had then believed, to the little triple waterfall where the plants with clover-shaped leaves big as dinner plates grew, had stated that he was heading towards an area of lower ground. So she must now be treading those last few miles.

But on the following day, shortly after they had resumed their march after a midday rest and meal, a change in the nature of the Forest began to manifest itself. The great towering trees were at ever-increasing distances from one another. The sky above was no longer only to be glimpsed through tiny bright-blue diamond windows. Instead there were larger and larger patches through which the sunlight came slanting down in huge dusty white swathes. Where they fell the pleasant coolness was turned in an instant into areas of steamy heat.

Then, ahead, she saw a palm tree, and soon another and another.

Before very much longer, while she was still debating with herself whether this change in the terrain was a good or bad thing, the Forest rapidly petered out altogether. In front of them stretched a wide lake of gingery-green swamp.

At its edge a few palms grew. Away to the left there was a belt of trees Thomasina recognised from her time at the coast as Candelabra Screw-pines. She had always thought they were much more like palms than pines, but, call them what you would, she knew they were to be avoided. Their aerial roots formed networks so interlaced that getting past them was a virtual impossibility. Their long sword-shaped leaves, too, had spiny edges that could cut clothes as viciously as if they had been ripped with scissors. To the right, she saw, the swamp curved away till it was lost from sight.

She took a bearing from the compass secured to her waist. Then she turned to Fito.

"No help for it," she said. "We will have to go through it, straight ahead."

Fito, his face a picture of lugubriousness, said nothing.

"No," she answered his unspoken declaration, "I must go on. The plant that I have come all this way to take back is there. On the far side. The best plant for healing in all the Forest."

Still Fito said nothing.

Thomasina wondered whether to attempt to explain about Doctor Diver's notes and how they had said that patches of swamp were to be found on the last day but one before he had come across the triple waterfall and the plants at its foot. But it had been difficult enough to explain to Manyalibo, with all his intelligence, what writing was, and Fito was by no means as clever.

She gave up the notion. Especially, she thought, since it would also involve explaining to Fito that the years between Doctor Diver's visit and this moment must have seen the transformation of his 'patches of swamp' into this unbroken area in front of them. So she would not only have to convey to Fito what writing did, but she would have to go

162

on to say that sometimes the knowledge which writing had so carefully preserved could be made useless by the changes brought by time to the ever-changing Forest.

No, there was nothing for it but to command.

She pointed to the swamp, its greeny-black water scummed over with ginger and broken here and there by plants whose pale stems reached up and fell back in curves of weird gracefulness. Further across there were clumps of palms to be seen, their elegant fronds reflected in the utterly still surface.

Perhaps these indicated that the whole was not impossibly deep.

"Go in," she said to Fito. "Go in, and see how deep it is. See if you can find where it is safe to walk."

Fito said nothing.

He had put down the folded Wardian case and the small bundle of other essential items he had carried for her for so long. He made no effort to pick them up again.

Thomasina looked up at the sun. There must be three hours of daylight left still, she calculated. There ought to be time to reach the far side of the swamp where she could just make out a dim thicker density of green, the beginning again of the Forest proper. But there was not going to be any moving Fito. That she could see from the stubborn stillness with which he was holding himself, if from nothing else.

She gave a long sigh.

"We will stay where we are for the night," she said.

At once Fito lost the look of obstinate dejection that had been planted on his customarily half-smiling face. He bent and picked up his burdens, carried them back to the edge of the Forest behind them and began to gather wood for a fire.

Oh ho, my lad, Thomasina said to herself, you believe we're going to set off back home tomorrow, do you not? Well, you can jolly well think again. Tomorrow you and I are going to make our way across that swamp. If we have to go under to our very heads to do so. Either that, or there's going to be a parting of the ways. Because, nothing, nothing at all, is going to stop me finding my dead old friend's life-giving plant. Nothing. Nothing. Nothing.

CHAPTER 15

Major Jacky had halted the column well before the time darkness fell.

"No point in any forced marching," he had said cheerfully to David. "Keep the men fresh. Never know when trouble may crop up in rainforest and one will need one's full resources to press forward."

"Yes. That is, no. No, I suppose not."

So the elaborate business of setting up camp had been put in hand. Hammocks were strung between convenient trees, and at decent distances from one another. The porters built themselves a huge fire and, their duties over, cooked themselves a meal at it. Old N'goi, seemingly as happy with one of Major Jacky's portable stoves as he had been with anything else he had cooked on, produced one of his semi-European suppers.

"I suppose he learnt from some Belgian empire-builder long ago," David had commented. "But I'm sure it wasn't for cooking he picked us up that day in the market."

"Then why did he, that's what I'd like to know," Tom had answered. "I don't believe he did it by magic either, whatever you say."

"No soul, that's your trouble, Mountjoy."

"Too much imagination, that's yours, Teigh. It's why you're so bloody jumpy about the Forest."

"Jumpy? Well, all right, I suppose you could call it that. If you were devoid of all sympathetic feelings. But I prefer to see it as the actual realisation of what me old mate Conrad called the horror, the horror."

After the meal was over and the petromax lamps lit Major Jacky took them both aside, with a faintly conspiratorial air.

"A word with you chaps, if I may."

"We're all ears," David said.

Major Jacky shot him a sharp look out of cobalt-blue eyes.

"Yes, Jacky?" Tom said quickly. "What can we do for you?"

Major Jacky gave his right calf one firm whack with his stick.

"It's more what you can do for yourselves, actually," he said. "It's about your Mr Lunn."

"Tom Gunn, oh God," David said.

"Lunn. Yes. Well, as I warned you at the start, the fellow's becoming a first-class nuisance. I caught him attempting to wander off just now. In the dark. Total lack of discipline."

"Yes, well," Tom said, "I'm afraid that's the way it is with him."

"Yes. But this is what it's all about. I mean, you chaps want him to guide us to this cairn thing, don't you? And, to tell the truth, I'm pretty concerned that we're going to find he's no longer with us before we get anywhere near the target area. So what I propose is this. Of course, I've posted sentries all round, but I can't expect my fellows, sterling chaps though they are, to put your Mr Lunn under close arrest if they spot him making off. So what it amounts to is: I think your group better make yourselves responsible for keeping the fellow under strict surveillance."

"But, good God -"

"No, Teigh," Tom broke in, "I do see Jacky's point. I know it's not what we might like doing but I think we've just got to."

David gave her a look that clearly signalled they would discuss it all later – and she would row back on her decision. But he said nothing.

"Well then, that's settled. Good show. And I'll leave you to make out your own roster, David."

Major Jacky marched away.

Tom turned to David.

"We'll do all the sentry-go between the two of us," she said with sharp insistence. "Josh would be just as liable as Tim Lunn to wander off, and Reg would complain it's against the union regulations."

"Well, yes, but -"

"I'll take first watch, and then I'll wake you at – what? – 2 AM?"

"First watch? First watch? Christ, you've certainly fallen under the magical spell of the demon-lover of Canopforce. Next thing you

165

know you'll be writing some military-style journal tosh – Sergeant Teigh was detailed to take second watch - "

"You'd better get some sleep now," Tom replied coldly. "If we're going to be walking through the Forest all tomorrow you'll need all your energy. Especially as it'll probably take you half the night to get into that hammock."

And David, to his fizzing chagrin, did find clambering into a hammock ridiculously difficult.

***

When Tom woke David at two she told him that Tim Lunn was not asleep.

"I think he never does more than catnap anyhow," she said.

"He sits there propped up against the buttress of that tree, and every half hour or so he gets up and wanders around."

"Christ, is he really going to make tracks? Don't tell me Major Jacky's got it right?"

"No I think he's probably safe enough. He hasn't shown any signs of leaving up to now anyhow. But I'd watch him."

"Oh God, why do things like this have to happen to me?"

"Because they're a just reward for your incorrigible idleness and your disordered life."

With infuriating ease Tom swung herself up into her hammock and adjusted the waterproof sheet above it. A dismissive tent.

So it was with very mixed feelings that, about an hour later, David thrust his head under that same waterproof sheet and shone his flashlight on to Tom's face.

"Wha - what is it?"

"It's Tim Lunn. He's disappeared."

In an instant Tom was fully awake. Her eyes, bright marbles in the torch's light, glared back at David.

"What do you mean disappeared?"

"He's – he's gone. I'm sorry. I dozed off for a bit, and when something woke me – a bloody great drop of water from a tree – I

166

realised old Tom Gunn had vanished."

"Have you looked for him? He's probably only gone for a pee. And don't call him Tom Gunn."

"Yes. Yes, I have looked. Everywhere. I even asked Major Jacky's bloody sentry, and he said Tom - bloody Lunn had walked past him about a quarter of an hour before."

Tom had already rolled neatly up into a sitting position in the hammock. She grabbed the boots she had left, in accordance with Major Jacky's 'standing orders', at the hammock's end safe from scorpions and started thrusting her feet into them.

"We'll have to go and find him," she said. "God, if Jacky discovers we've let him get away he'll cancel the whole sodding expedition."

"But how can we find him? It's dark. Pitch dark. And we're in the middle of a bloody jungle. Nowhere goes anywhere. How can we possibly find someone in all that?"

"Oh don't be so wet. We'll ask the sentry which way he went. And the old bugger's probably got a light with him. We'll spot that. After all, he won't be able to see in the dark any more than we can."

"I suppose not."

Miserably David followed her.

And, yes, the sentry said, the old man had taken a bush-light from the fire. He had gone that way.

They set out in the same direction.

The Forest was instantly black all around them. The beam of their flashlight seemed only to make things worse. It picked out a giant tree-trunk here, a torrent of descending lianas there. Then its light showed another tree-trunk that might have been the first one once more. Or another tumbling cascade of creeper that was different from the earlier one and yet hard to remember in what way.

When they had left, the path which the sentry had pointed out had seemed plain enough. But the moment they were beyond the glow from the camp's shrouded fire all signs of any track were swallowed up in the darkness.

But there was no difficulty in making their way forward. Indeed, the difficulty was precisely in the choice of ways that confronted them. Major Jacky had chosen to bivouac in a particularly clear area. Between the trunks of the trees there was plenty of open ground. It was yielding and squelchy underfoot, but it in no way impeded progress. Even the huge bunches of lianas clung close to the trunks of the trees and presented no obstacle.

"Christ, Tom," David said after a little, "we're probably going round in a circle. We'll never find him at this rate."

"Do you want to go back then, wake Major Jacky and tell him what you've done?"

David made no answer.

A minute or so later he exclaimed "oh, why does life have to be so awful?"

Tom did not offer any explanation.

They floundered on.

"I used to go for walks in the woods at night when I was a kid," David said, after several long minutes of silence. "I used to actually climb out of my bedroom window. It wasn't very difficult, as a matter of fact. And then I'd go for a wander in the wood at the back of the house. I used to love it. It was romantic. Fucking romantic. I'd give myself the jimjams thinking about witches and wizards, and even wolves I suppose. And I'd come back exhilarated. Exhilarated."

He paused for a moment, and tramped ploddingly onwards.

"But this," he said. "This. God, no one could give themselves the comfortable willies in this. It isn't even eerie. It's inconceivable. Impossible."

"Well, it's certainly impossible to listen for old Tom Gunn with you wittering on like that."

For half a minute David was silent. The sharp smell of chlorophyll alternated in their nostrils with danker odours from the decaying debris they were treading underfoot.

"And anyhow," David grated abruptly into the darkness, "you said he wasn't to be called Tom Gunn."

"Oh, shut up. Just shut up, and keep your ears open."

Again they marched along without speaking. Tom, who had taken charge of the flashlight, turned its beam this way and that. It never penetrated very far, and all that it ever showed them was yet another tree-trunk, erect, towering, bare.

"And anyhow what's the use of keeping one's ears open?" David said "listen to that bloody noise everything's making. We wouldn't hear Tom - Tim Lunn, blast him, if he was singing his ruddy soul out."

It was true the night Forest was noisier than the day. There was an unending chorus of frogs, a pink-pink-pinking that rapidly got on the nerves. There were mysterious gruntings, sometimes all too close at hand. There was a coughing noise, plainly not human, that might have come from a leopard. There were insect squawkings and churrings in a never-ceasing background. Occasionally from high above, just perceptible, there was the thin high-pitched whine emitted by some hunting bat.

Then from not far away, there came a long, sad, rasping cry, echoey and despairing.

"What - for Christ's sake, what was that?" David said.

"Rock-badger, hyrax," Tom answered tersely. "I read about them in Thomasina's note-book. And so did you."

"Well, I dare say I did. But, delightful writer though Thomasina was in many ways, she never got near describing the ghostliness of that. And it isn't a nice ghostliness either."

On they went, tramping, peering, listening without much hope. Neither was willing to be the first to say their search had failed. From time to time moths attempted to immolate themselves against the flashlight's glass. They were bigger, by far, than any moth either of them had ever seen before.

It was Tom who eventually came to a full halt. "It's no use," she said. "We're not going to find him. And, besides, the bugger's probably back sitting propped against his tree, happy as Larry."

"But if he's not..."

"Then we'll just have to confess to Major Jacky. He'll find out in any case when he wakes up in an hour or two. Perhaps he'll organise another of his recces. With more success this time."

"Yes. Perhaps."

David swung round and started to tramp back in the direction they had come. Tom, still wielding the torch, stepped up to walk at his side. It was as dark as ever and the noises of the night had not slackened. From time to time a mosquito would come whining in to the attack.

"Oh God," David said, slapping his bare arm, "we'll have to ask Major Jacky for something from his medicine chest."

"More lectures," Tom said. "As if we won't be getting enough."

They walked on in increasingly depressed silence.

It was only when they had been going for what they both had come to realise was a good deal longer than the outward search had taken that they stopped suddenly by mutual consent.

For a long time they stood without speaking. Neither seemed willing to state aloud the fact that plainly they were lost.

"Well, what do we do?" David asked at last.

"I don't know," Tom said. "Try casting round to see if we recognise anything? Sit tight and wait for daylight?"

"Recognise anything? In this?"

"Well, no. I suppose it's just wait then."

"At least daylight will come. That's the one thing we can be sure of. About the only thing."

"Yes."

Tom flopped down against the bole of the nearest tree. David, more cautiously, lowered himself beside her. Tom put out the flashlight.

It seemed a long time till the deep darkness all around began to yield to the greeny gloom of the Forest day. But at last the cicadas set up their dawn churring and the shape of the trees began to become visible.

They stood up and peered in every direction.

But wherever they looked the Forest seemed exactly the same. Here and there rays from the rising sun penetrated in long, thin, ice-smoky beams. But, since they had no idea where relative to the east Major Jacky's camp was, the sight was no help. Nor could they see very far when it was fully daylight. The green murk swiftly curtailed vision, and the huge trunks of the trees one behind the other with their thickly dangling lianas all too soon formed an impenetrable screen.

"Reniforms, falciforms, luniforms," David said.

"What? What's that?"

"Just quoting. Thomasina. On the shapes of those bloody creepers."

"Well, don't. We're lost. Lost. Try thinking about that."

"Yes, sorry, love. Bit frivolous, I admit. But I don't know what we can do. I suppose we could try giving a shout from time to time. Major Jacky's no doubt deploying search parties. Each with an appropriate name."

"Don't rubbish him either. You'll be bloody glad he has got some notion of doing things in an orderly way when his searchers find us."

She gave David a sparking glare.

"If they ever do find us," she added.

"Well, let's shout anyhow."

They shouted at intervals for perhaps a quarter of an hour, and then for as long again at less and less frequent intervals. But the Forest seemed to absorb their voices. It drowned them in its ocean of silence. A silence broken only by the unending churring of the cicadas that seemed no more than an element of that silence.

"What's going to happen to us then?" David said at last.

Tom took a moment or two to think.

"Well," she said eventually, "it's like this. Either Jacky's search parties find us, or they don't. If they do, end of unpleasant situation. If they don't, I suppose we try to find something to eat and we drink some of this rainwater, never mind possible dysentery, and we somehow carry on for a bit. Or... or, we don't. Finish. Goodbye. Curtains."

"But it can't be like that," David exploded. "I mean, for God's sake, this is the twentieth century. Two people can't just die in the middle of the African rainforest, with a whole expedition within a couple of miles of them. They can't."

"But they could," Tom said. "In all this confusion and mess it's by no means impossible that no one will ever find us, however well organised the search is. Make up your mind to that."

David groaned.

"But I love you," he said.

"Yes, well, come to that, I love you too. But that isn't reason enough for us to be found."

"I wish there was a God," David said, after a short silence. "I wish there was a God hovering up there, just waiting for a few really penitent prayers and then sweeping into action. Producing Major Jacky and his merry men in five minutes flat."

"I know what you mean. But we don't have those sorts of certainties. Not like Thomasina did."

"And she didn't, not after she's been in the Forest a few months. There's no talk about God or Providence, capital P, in her diaries after a bit."

"Damn, blasted, fucking diaries. Why did we ever see them?"

"God, Tom, if we ever get out of this, I'll be good for ever more. I'll remember that I said I would, too. I swear it. I will spend the rest of my life doing the right thing – whatever that is."

"I expect it's getting married, having children, keeping a steady job. It's probably me not having a job, steady or otherwise, and just looking after the little housie."

David gave a rather woebegone smile.

"I don't think it's come to that," he said. "I mean, I don't think you need promise all that."

"Not to getting married?"

"Well, I meant not to the housie. I'm not sure about the marriage bit. I mean, if... well, if we ever do get back to dear old England, safe and well and happily editing away at the film, well, do you think we ought to get married in a proper way?"

"If I say yes now, it'll only be because I'm dead scared."

"Yeah, I know. Do you think we ought to start walking? In some direction?"

"We'd only most likely be heading away from Major Jacky and his search parties just as fast as they were heading towards us. If they are."

"Fucking Forest."

CHAPTER 16

A night's sleep had done nothing to infuse Fito with courage. Thomasina knew it as soon as she woke and saw him. He was standing looking out at the lake of cotton-woolly mist that was covering the swamp. A thick tendril of it was lapping over his big, flat, bare feet. His shoulders were hunched in an attitude of utter obstinacy.

She lay where she was for a little, wondering what she should do.

One thing was clear. She was not going to give up her quest. Not after she had come so many hundreds of miles and was within a day, or two at the most, of reaching its end.

But could she succeed in persuading Fito to cross the swamp?

Would shouted commands urge him on enough? She could hardly beat him into obeying, though she had a notion that if she tried he would submit to it uncomplainingly. But still he would not be moved. That was plain even from the angle of his hunched bare shoulders, just catching the morning sun, gleaming with oil and unwashed-off sweat.

So could she manage without his help? She had sworn last evening that, if it came to it, she would. But that had been in a rage. Now, looking at things rationally, was it going to be possible to traverse that great acreage of swamp entirely without assistance?

If she did, if she could contrive it, she had no doubt that she could accomplish the rest of her mission without difficulty. She had, after she had become Manyalibo's pupil, often enough spent time on her own in the Forest. She knew its way well enough now to have no fears about finding that triple waterfall, and, with the healing plant safe, making her journey back to the far edge of the swamp. And then, if she had crossed that ominous sucking area once, she could surely do so again in the opposite direction.

But would she be able to get across in the first place?

All at once she decided that she would. She must. She would make the attempt, even if it meant that she perished in it. Even death in that passage of trial would not be as terrible an end as it would have been had she died of fever when she had first come to Manyalibo's village or had the leopard that had killed M'bene taken her life instead. Dying in this last attempt would make sense of her whole life. It would endow it with purpose.

She jumped up.

"Fito, breakfast," she called.

It was one of the English words she had introduced him to.

He turned towards her. His customary soft slight smile was already beginning to come back to his face. All that his shoulders had said was being contradicted.

"Be-fas," he echoed.

It did not take him long to encourage embers of their fire to life and to make tea on it from the last remains of the supply she had brought to Africa with her. Her last link, almost, with civilisation.

She drank with warm contentment. Her mind now was fully made up. She ate, too, her full share of agouma cake, rich and sweet. She would need all the sustenance she could get.

Fito, poor Fito, she suspected was convinced she was going to do the sensible thing and had given up any mad idea of crossing a place as dangerous as the swamp, so filled with bad juju.

Well, he would soon learn differently.

The moment he began gathering up their scanty possessions she put it to him squarely.

"Fito are you coming?"

He turned and gave the swamp one quick scared look. The sun had dispersed the mist and its gingery-green surface stood revealed in all its menace.

"Come home, come home," he said with pleading plaintiveness.

"Oh, no," Thomasina answered, in the English he could not understand, well though he was able to gather its import. "Here we part, my friend. Take what you need to go your way. But leave me the

Wardian case, my tea canister, my memoranda books. I am for the swamp, let it do what it will."

***

Old N'goi found Tom and David. He came up to them out of the Forest as simply as he had appeared at their table in the bar Vatican the first time they had seen him. His washed-out pink singlet seemed suddenly softly to materialise in the pervasive green light.

David was the first to realise he was there. He shook Tom, who was sitting at the base of the tree where they had been all along, her head on her knees.

"Look. Look. Look who's here again."

He jumped up and ran towards the old man.

"N'goi. N'goi. It's you. You. Where are the others? The search parties? I mean, ou sont les autres?"

"Je suis venu tout seul, m'sieu."

Tom, evidently having as much difficulty as David in believing they were seeing what they were, joined in the interrogation.

"Et Monsieur Lunn? Le vieux? Est-ce qu'on l'a trouvé? Lui aussi?"

"Il n'a pas disparu, Madame. Il est toujours chez nous."

Old N'goi looked at them with his habitual impassiveness.

"On me dit que vous n'étiez pas la," he said in his unexpectedly lucid French. "Ainsi je suis venu moi-meme vous conduire aux autres."

Tom looked at David.

"Well," she said, "I suppose I've got to believe in those magic powers now."

"More than that," David said. "You've got to lead a decent, regular life when we get back. You promised. Marriage, children, the little housie."

***

Thomasina entered the swamp as soon as Fito's lithe bare back had been swallowed up into the Forest behind her. Near where they had spent the night a few black rocks seemed to rise above the green and black water. They seemed, too, to run more or less in a line. She hoped they indicated a way across the wide, almost featureless stretch, a path of sorts that would keep her reasonably out of its sucking grasp.

For a quarter of an hour or more she did seem to be able to make her way forward with the blackish ginger-topped mud doing little more than drag the hem of her skirt. She would have liked to have been able to walk with her skirt held above that deceptive surface. But she now had to carry the Wardian case on her head, in Fito's manner, as well as holding in her hand the leather bag containing her few other possessions.

After a while she found that any hopes she had had of keeping her clothes relatively clean must be abandoned. The line of rock underneath the surface of the water had gradually sunk lower. The thickly oozy mud was creeping correspondingly higher. At last it was up to the level of her knees, and the going had become fearfully hard. At each step she had to lean far forward to drag her mud-laden skirt onwards. But she saw nothing else but that to do.

Ahead the swamp stretched out, seeming never to lessen in the distance still to be got through. The line of darker green, which she took to be the beginning of the Forest proper once again, appeared always to be so far off that reaching it seemed impossibly removed. Only when she allowed herself a look backwards was she a little comforted by the increasing distance of the Forest out of which she and Fito had come.

Then, gradually, she began to find that the stuff through which she was wading was becoming less mud-like, more watery. She told herself she was making better progress. But she was aware, too, quaveringly aware, that the footing under her was patently more treacherous.

Almost the only feature to break the level monotony, beside the occasional graceful swamp flower rising up from the ooze, was a clump of palms. It lay, so far as she could judge, directly on the path made for her by the rocks below. Now it was, she hoped, no more than three hundred yards away. She fixed her eyes on it, and resolved to reach it without once faltering. In its shelter, she told herself, she

176

could cling to one of the slender trunks and take the rest she longed to have.

And, hardly had she formed the resolve, than she fell full length.

Her foot had slipped into a cleft between two of the invisible rocks below and had been caught there. For a moment she had swayed helplessly and then she had fallen. The thick black stuff, hardly water, not altogether mud, had closed right over her. Before she had sense enough to shut her mouth tight she had taken in a foul mouthful of it.

Lashing wildly round her, she made contact again with the more solid ground. Bodily she pulled herself towards it. And at last, wriggling, heaving and squirming, she succeeded in getting fully back on to it. And eventually she pushed herself to her feet.

She spat the disgusting stuff from her mouth. She breathed deeply in. She had at last the strength to look about her.

And there was the Wardian case, not destroyed, not sunk in the black mud past all retrieving. Instead it had come to rest apparently on the edge of the rocky path she had been following, sticking up on its side. She stooped, hauled it free of the thick slime and examined it. Its thick glass had survived. It was dirty, but totally intact. Into it, if only the rest of the swamp could be got over without worse mishap, eventually Doctor Diver's miracle-working plants could be put.

She set out again. It took her an hour under the beating-down sun to reach the clump of palms she had set her sights on just before her fall. But reach it she did. There the period of rest she had promised herself, almost embracing the trunk of one of the five slender trees, did her good.

But it took her until the sun was within two hours of reaching the horizon before at last she staggered on to firm ground on the far side, weary in every limb, covered from blouse top to skirt hem in black filth. Then, frankly sobbing with relief – it was the first occasion in all her months in Africa that she had allowed tears to fall – she saw, as she had failed to see before, that round her exposed neck there was a collar of black, clinging leeches.

She gritted her teeth. The gorging creatures would take not a little removing. In her early days in the Forest she had on occasion attracted the attention of two or three of them at a time, but then she had had a steady supply of salt and it had not been too difficult to get rid of them. Now it would be a matter of squeezing and tugging and enduring some sharp pain.

She set to work.

And, eventually, not without feeling faint from loss of blood, she was free of the creatures and ready to enter the blessed cool of the Forest once more. She had, she calculated, not much more than an hour before she would need to find somewhere safe and comfortable to sleep. So, giving up any notion of getting the mud out of her clinging clothes, she reached for the compass from its strap at her waist, wiped its face and took a bearing.

And, yes, she saw, she had kept a true line right across the miasma of the swamp.

She smiled.

It was, it must be, a good omen.

And, within ten minutes of entering the Forest, another omen of success greeted her. At the foot of the third giant tree she passed, cradled between two of its great, snail-like buttresses, there was a pool of the finest clearest water.

A bath-tub, she thought. A gift to wash away all the mud and the blood. The Forest is offering me its kindest hospitality.

***

The long file marched on. At its head, the two machete men slashed away any winding creeper or bush that might impede progress. After them came Jacky Yombton-Smith, a constant cheerful grin on his ruddy, blue-eyed face, compass in hand, occasionally consulted. There followed the line of porters, their different but equal loads resting easily on their heads, food supplies, bedding rolls, folded tables, chairs. Towards the end David, Tom, Reg and Josh had their places. Almost at the last old N'goi loped along, a flitting pink vest in the greenish twilight. And, still keeping some twenty yards to the rear, there was the shabby, Crusoe figure of Tim Lunn, with them but not of them, totally uncaring of the alarm he had created the night before.

Tom turned her head back to David.

"You see that tree? The one you can just make out ahead and to the left?"

"Palm, isn't it? Not really my idea of proper primeval jungle, I must say. More your oriental lasciviousness."

"No. Do you know what it means?"

"Oh God, not philosophy. The deeper meaning of the palm-tree."

Tom turned back again to shoot him a look of mock fury.

"It means, idiot, that where we are now was once, in all probability, an area of swamp."

"Geography lesson much app - hey, you're telling me that this was where Thomasina ploughed through that swamp? Up to her elbows in black mud? Leeches – what was it? – *in a collar round her neck?*"

"That's it. So, for one thing, shouldn't you be getting Reg to shoot some film? It's interesting, the changes that take place over the years in the rainforest. The way just one enormous tree falling can block a stream, start of swampy patch. Or do the opposite, create some drainage. End of swamp. As here, maybe.

"Well, yes, interesting enough, I admit. Though I do wish you'd stop saying rainforest. I don't want this film to become just one more ecology freaks' masturbatory fantasy."

"Oh, bloody primeval jungle to you."

But, despite the taunt, David hurried on ahead and asked Major Jacky for a short halt for Reg to get his camera to work.

"And don't make it too arty," he told Reg, after he had squinted at the palm-tree in the viewfinder.

"I think you can rely on me for that. I can get a straight shot on film when I'm asked to."

"Yes, I know. Sorry, Reg. I've a great regard for your ability, old man."

Then he spoilt it.

"And that's actually true," he added, with surprise. "I don't know why, but the longer we've been on this mad jaunt the more I appreciate people who just get things done."

"I don't see that it's a mad jaunt at all," Reg said. "I think it'll turn out a nice, interesting little film. Just the sort of thing Mrs. Blandy likes of an evening."

"Yes. Yes. Well – er – carry on then. You won't need me, will you?"

"I can manage, thank you."

David crept away to confide in Tom how, once again, he had mishandled Reg.

"But, Christ," he said, "if that man tells me once more that this is going to be a nice little film that Mrs. Blandy will grant her approval to, I'll stuff his sodding camera down his sodding throat."

"Now, now. Remember David Teigh, when we get back home you and I have promised to become Mr And Mrs. Yes? To settle down in our little housie? I expect there'll be nothing I'll like better than a good nature film on telly."

"Oh, God, Tom, we don't have to do that, do we? I mean, a promise under threat isn't really a promise. Is it?"

"You swore to be a good boy for ever and ever."

"Well, all right, I did. But if you're faced with actual, positive death it's only natural to hope to see yourself live to lead a better life. And, in any case, I don't think we were living all that awful a life before."

"Living in sin. That's what it was."

"Now, come off it. You can only live in sin if you believe it's a sin to live in sin. We had a good solid relationship. Mutual benefit, and all that. And, thanks to the almighty pill, no risk of bringing poor unwanted children into the world. Nothing wrong there. Nothing at all."

"No, I know. I mean, we even talked about that, when we began. But..."

Tom looked down at the soggy ground at her feet.

"No," David said, with more than a little vehemence. "Damn it, we were all right then. We're all right now. We're pledged to each other, aren't we? In love, for God's sake. It means just as much, more, more than if we'd paraded and ponced about in a church, you all in white, me in bloody morning dress."

"Yeah... yeah, I know it does, Teigh. But... but, well, being there, lost like that, it did actually bring it home to me. Like how long will love last? And has it, really, all the time been just lust? All of that."

"Well, it isn't just lust. You know it isn't."

"Yes, I do know. And I believe it too. But, all the same, I still can't help asking myself sometimes – well, now especially – will it last? Properly last? Till death do us...?"

"I don't see why not. Well, I haven't ever really thought about it before. But I don't see why not."

"But I don't see why, either. Okay, we get on well. We have done for three whole years. And the sex is great. Fine. But is there any reason why it should all go on being like it has?"

"All right. But do you think standing in a church and promising funny things like 'with my body I thee worship' is going to make a difference?"

"Oh, I don't know. It might. It somehow might. I mean, not promising to a God we neither of us happen to believe in, but the actual making of promises. In public, if you like"

"Well, Jesus, isn't that just submitting to some sort of moral blackmail? Or appealing to our pride even? I mean, I don't think much of a promise if what's making you keep it is the fear of what all the people you made it in front of will say."

Tom shot him a sudden, sullen glance.

"Then I gather you're no longer proposing to me? As you've been doing at intervals since before we even came to Africa?"

"Well... well, yes, you do gather, I suppose. I did sort of want you to marry me. But – oh, I don't know – it was a sort of frivolous idea. A kind of joke, really."

"Oh, thank you."

"No. No, Tom, I mean, I did mean it. But... but, well, it was not exactly a joke but sort of play-acting. Though I did mean what I was saying. If you'd said okay, I'd have done it. Cheerfully. But, now... well, I sort of feel different. That I mustn't make jokes like that. You said it, too, the other day. Something about being challenged. Do you think it's what Africa does to you?"

"A dread disease? Well, if it's that, I suppose you could throw it off.

181

Back home. Or here, with a few jabs from Major Jacky's medical kit."

"Yeah, but I'm afraid this is one of the incurable ones. Moral Aids. You know, it was the night in the Forest that finally did it. Like the man said, almost: when you know you're going to starve to death in a fortnight it concentrates the mind wonderfully. I suppose, then, I did really see marriage as more than just getting married. I saw it as being all that."

"All what? I'm not with you. And anyhow, what man?"

"What man?"

"Who said about starving and concentrating the mind."

"Oh. Oh, yes. Dr Johnson. I suppose you've never heard of him? And it was being hanged. But starving to death is just as good. So I discovered. Makes you realise that something like marriage is putting yourself into the bloody order of things. Something like that."

"Yes. Yes, I see that. And I have heard of Dr Johnson."

"That's something, I suppose. But the thing is, the really awful thing, that if getting married is all that, then I'm not sure I want to do it. Ever."

"No, I see. It is asking a lot, I see that."

Again Tom looked at the squelchy ground. She bit her lip.

"God," David said, "wouldn't it be nice to believe in God? In the whole hierarchy of it? Everything in its place. Arch-angels, angels, saints, plain mortals, animals, trees, stones. All beautifully arranged. I mean, to believe in archangels..."

"Teigh... we're not joking."

"No, I mean it. Well, not about archangels. But I think I almost do believe how marvellous it would be if one believed in the system. If we knew we had to do what we had been told to do. Thou shalt not commit adultery, honour thy father and mother, the lot. It'd all be so simple then."

"Well, actually, I don't think it would. I don't think it really was for people when they did believe in that. Or when they felt they ought to. I think it must have been just as difficult for them as for us now. Life is difficult."

"Well, yes. Yes, I suppose it always was."

"And, in any case, it's not possible to believe just because you want to. Just because you feel you're sliding about everywhere, and don't like it. You know that."

"Oh, God, yes. Yes, I do. But why does life always have to be so complicated and confusing?"

"Because it is life, you poor old thing. Because that's what life is."

***

I must have been lying for above a quarter of an hour in my pool of clear rainwater held between that mighty tree's buttresses, letting the swamp mud slip from my limbs, soothing my neck after the attentions of that collar of leeches, hardly thinking any thoughts, when I became aware I was not, as I had believed, alone. Alone, of course, save for the ever-present million insects and in the leafy heaven above the monkeys and the birds, busy at their tasks of food gathering, of combining with the flowers in the high tree world to procreate and spread their seed, of mating in that endless round of life renewal and death concluding that is the Forest's existence. I was being watched from where my buttress screens did not protect me by other eyes than these. I had been so, I knew at once, for almost as long as I had bathed in the tub which nature had so conveniently filled for me.

I rolled round in the clear, lapping water. And I saw him. I have come to call him Atembogunjo, the name he tells me he had before he left his village. He was as naked as I was myself, and his virile member was as erect as those of the apes I have seen mating in the Forest – that sight which when I first came upon it those many months ago disturbed me so greatly. But all such false modesty I have long ago lost. More, I responded to Atembogunjo. I, who had thought that having reached my thirtieth year I was never to experience that fever, more terrible than any of the fevers I have endured in the Forest, that fever called love, responded in lightning-flash, come-from-nowhere immediacy.

So it was that my different life began. My life with Atembogunjo.

How strange that, turning the page to set down a new sentence, I find I have come to the very end of this memoranda book, the sixth I have filled since writing those words, as I remember them, 'This morning I smelt Africa'. Yet it is strangely fitting that now I should have to commence a new volume. I am commencing a new life, a different, altogether unexpected life, which will yet, I am certain, be mine for as long as I shall live now. It will be fully the life that the Forest has slowly and insidiously taught me to live. It is, surely, the meaning hidden and obscure, of all that has happened to me since I first stepped among the towering trees. My life with Atembogunjo.

CHAPTER 17

Chapter 14: Diversionary Tactics by Major J.F.Yombton-Smith

Once the errant Mr Lunn had returned to camp Alcott, I considered there was nothing that should further delay Operation Diarieshunt. Indeed, the sooner we sallied forth the better. Otherwise our sole guide to the place where Thomasina le Mesurier had, according to Mr Peter Brentiswood-Jones (with whom I had the most satisfactory dealings from start to finish), placed the remaining volumes of her journal, this guide was quite likely to depart once again for a destination unknown.

One whole day was therefore allocated to making ready, on the old principle that one ounce of preparation is worth a pound of subsequent disaster. Yet even over this necessary task I encountered a certain amount of trouble. Mr Lunn, who made himself a wretched nuisance while I was ensuring that my men each had equal loads to carry and were a hundred percent fit foot-wise (very important) created a certain amount of stress and strain. That was perhaps to be expected. But Mr David Teigh I found also clearly believed that all the hard work my fellows and I were putting in was unnecessary. Had it been left to him, we would have set forth the very morning after Mr Lunn had been retrieved from his wandering in the rainforest. But, frankly, I was not prepared to countenance any operation not conducted on proper military lines, especially as I had come to realise that Filmforce had undergone no acclimatisation procedure whatsoever. Nor had any of its personnel much notion of rainforest discipline.

I had further discovered, not to mince words, that Mr Teigh, whom I had assumed to be i/c Filmforce, by no means saw himself in any such position of authority. I had begun to get an inkling of this state of affairs, in fact, within a few minutes of Filmforce's arrival at base camp by river transport. In the course of my initial briefing to the party I had occasion to notice Miss Mountjoy deliver to Mr Teigh what I can only describe as a quick kick to the shin. That was, to be perfectly blunt, something no officer of more senior rank should have permitted, even if there were other relations between them, as it soon became evident was the case with Miss Mountjoy, or 'Tom' as she was good enough to ask me to call her, and Mr Teigh.

I am well aware, of course, that in any force with mixed sex personnel complications are likely to arise. My view is that if persons wish to indulge in sexual relations, this is their privilege, always provided that these relations in no way jeopardise good order and discipline, i.e. provided in general that they do not cross the barrier between officer and other rank. I take a sterner view of fraternisation with the local populace where untold harm may be done. But I did not expect there to be many opportunities for this, if any, while Filmforce came under my general command. Otherwise I would have felt bound to have delivered a general pep talk on the dangers of v.d. plus Aids.

Altogether, then, I had formed the opinion before Operation Diarieshunt had properly taken off that Filmforce had been run up to that point of time, and was likely to be run in the future, in a thoroughly unmilitary manner. It would be idle, however, to pretend that much of life's business is conducted on military lines, and for much of the time there is, perhaps no reason why it should be. However, Filmforce was now about to embark on an operation which, though it was not planned to last for any great length of time, was nevertheless not without its potential dangers and difficulties. It is in such circumstances, in my opinion, that the military approach is mandatory. In no other way can hazards be reduced to the appropriate minimum.

This is hardly the place to hold forth on the military virtues, but a word or two may be permissible. A military training, as I see it, essentially provides one's life with purpose. One is dedicated to one aim and object, to making oneself into, or allowing oneself to be made into, the complete fighting man. When in initial training that object has been accomplished one is endowed thereafter with a continuing sense of purposefulness. I am aware, of course, that there is something of a paradox here, in that the purpose of a soldier is to fight wars and that for most of his career, in some instances in fact for the whole of an active career, there may be no wars to fight. Nevertheless the sense of purpose remains, and it can be dedicated to other spheres than the obviously military. It is, in fact, for that reason that I have entitled this book *Battle with the Rainforest*.

There is in this purposefulness, which is itself apt to make life particularly worthwhile, one factor that is of prime importance: obedience. Obedience is an unfashionable virtue in civilian circles in this day and age. But I believe the habit of obedience is well worth acquiring and pays considerable dividends in one's personal life, bitter though the bullet may be to bite upon – especially in one's training days. But obeying the orders of a superior officer unquestioningly and promptly means that there are removed from one all other options. The one remaining option, to carry out to the letter whatever order one has been given, can therefore be pursued with whole-hearted vigour. Much can thus be achieved.

However, this is to digress. To return to the narrative. Operation Diarieshunt commenced the following day at dawn. I am happy to say that in its initial stages everything went strictly according to plan. The whole force was ferried across the river that runs past Camp Alcott in our inflatable in precisely worked-out boatloads. On the far side I formed the party into single file, experience having taught me that this formation is by far the best way of marching in dense tropical or equatorial jungle. The only blemish on our first day's march was caused (again!) by Mr Lunn, who insisted on lingering at the rear of the column.

When we bivouacked, therefore, I thought it prudent to have a quiet word with Mr Teigh and 'Tom' Mountjoy, looking on them as a sort of joint command – not a practice I recommend – and suggesting that their group mount a night sentry roster for the purpose of ensuring Mr Lunn kept within bounds. Though I detected a certain amount of disaffection at the proposal, it was accepted.

I thought then that everything had been well taken care of and, after a very decent supper prepared by cook N'goi, I retired to my hammock for what I considered was some well-earned repose. It was only at reveille next morning that I discovered that not only had Mr Lunn been allowed to wander off during the hours of darkness but that Mr Teigh and 'Tom' Mountjoy had set off in pursuit and had failed to return.

Mr Lunn, I may say, had returned of his own accord well before first light. Worse, I found then that Mr Teigh in conducting his search had totally neglected the customary precaution of blazing convenient trees, as laid down in my standing orders. Consequently, there was no way of setting out on their trail with a view to discovering whether one or both of the party had fallen foul of some jungle hazard.

I immediately, therefore, organised a widespread search, deploying the men in groups of two in a wide circle round the bivouac site. However, they were unable to report any immediate success, a fact which will be more readily appreciated when it is remembered that in Rainforest visibility is seldom more than 20 metres and that the density of vegetation also deadens sound to a remarkable extent.

Several hours went by and I was beginning to have considerable fears for the safety of the missing pair. But then, to my surprise, accompanied only by cook N'goi they walked into the bivouac where I was maintaining HQ facilities. N'goi, it emerged in the course of debriefing, had come to the conclusion that my search parties were not going to meet with success and had thereupon, according to his own account, if I understood his French correctly, 'listened' until he knew exactly where in the surrounding rainforest the two lost Filmforce leaders were. He had then proceeded to fetch them. They returned, I may say, much bitten by mosquitoes, having failed to take proper precautions against this pest. A fate I felt to be richly deserved!

I leave it to my readers to assess the likelihood or otherwise of cook N'goi's accounts. Suffice it to say that I personally am prepared to accept it at face value. As the bard says 'there are more things in heaven and earth, Horatio...' whether there will ever be any military advantage in embodying local recruits with similar powers of 'seeing' or 'hearing' amid the flourishing confusion of equatorial jungle is a question that may perhaps be worth a certain amount of investigation.

In the circumstances our departure that day, the second of operation Diarieshunt, was delayed until after lunch had been taken, a meal again produced by cook N'goi with quiet efficiency. Consequently we made less progress than I had anticipated. However, a decent bivouac area was located well before the sudden onset of equatorial darkness, and on this occasion I did not hesitate to take security arrangements into my own hands, granting powers of arrest to the sentries I had posted.

Proper discipline having been established, our march thereafter was attended only by such vicissitudes as are to be expected in Rainforest. Twice we encountered columns of army ants, as described in my earlier chapter '*Military Operation in* Miniature'. On the second occasion, foreseeing a long delay while we waited for the column to go by, I gave the order for the construction of a bridge over the moving file of the vicious insects. Two trees were rapidly felled and with a little good honest hard work we were able to construct a bridge capable of carrying our whole party in safety. I may add that this was a matter of personal satisfaction to me in that Tim Lunn, whose constant boasting of his ability to move through rainforest with the minimum of tools and supplies had somewhat got on my nerves, was constrained eventually to make use of our bridge, constructed only because we had ready to hand and appropriately sorted an ample provision of axes, saws and rope!

Morale after that first night's unfortunate incident remained high. Indeed, on one occasion I felt it my duty to remonstrate with 'Tom' Mountjoy for an excess of care-freeness. She had declared to me that at last she was experiencing '*the timelessness, the irresponsibility and the freedom of the* Forest'. I was constrained to point out that irresponsibility is not a quality to be encouraged in rainforest conditions – or, I might have added, anywhere else.

However, our march continued at good speed, being enlivened at time with not a few moments of mirth. I particularly recall the occasion when the camera operator, Reg Blandy, in many ways a stalwart individual, while 'communing with nature' a short distance away from our bivouac was visited by a pair of highly inquisitive chimps and had to beat a hasty retreat in a state of partial undress.

So it was that at about 1200 hours on the sixth day of operation Diarieshunt we located our objective, having been guided on the final leg, I must admit, with considerable assurance and dash by my friend, Mr Lunn. The whole business of the opening of the cache where the diaries were in storage was eagerly recorded on film, and then, to my bewilderment, recorded once again from a different angle!

A good many of the 'shots', I understand, feature myself, though I have so far been unable to watch the completed film owing to a series of overseas postings. I am seen, however, I gather, pointing through the rainforest towards the cairn at the moment of our first sighting it, as well as later assisting 'Tom' Mountjoy to remove the ancient, mould-covered Gladstone bag in which Thomasina le Mesurier's precious memoranda books had been stored for so many years. Finally, I was delighted to go before the camera hoisting on an improvised flagstaff the Canopforce flag (unfortunately I had failed to get a Filmforce equivalent manufactured in time). I trust I appear to advantage!

CHAPTER 18

Tom extracted the last of the cardboard-covered memoranda books from the bottom of the mould-grey Gladstone bag that Thomasina le Mesurier had once carried for hundreds of miles through the Forest. She opened it and flipped through the pages of time-yellowed, thick paper.

"Blank," she said, her voice hollow with kept-back tears. "Blank like all the rest. Blank, blank, blank."

"Excuse me," Reg Blandy said, "but do you want me to go on filming, Dave? I mean, this isn't going to interest the viewers all that much is it? Not after what they were expecting."

"I am recording," Josh Perkins ground out. "Or I was. I was. But I'm not having off-mic cameraman's comment on my sound track."

"Oh, for God's sake," David said. "What does it matter? The chances are we're never going to see the film made now."

"Oh, I say, don't tell me that," Major Jacky exclaimed. "A chap was looking forward to Hollywood stardom."

He produced a chortling laugh.

No one paid him any attention. Tom let the last of the memoranda books drop to the musty black ground at her feet.

"I suppose we'll be able to cobble something together," she said. "But we'll be lucky to get a showing at some dead hour of the afternoon."

David bent to pick up the memoranda book from where it lay on the slimy layers of rotting forest debris, the long-ago fallen leaves, the insect bodies, the lizard corpses, the years-eroded bird bones.

And then he gave a little yelp.

"Hey, no, look," he said. "There is something written here. A page. No, two. Three. Right in the middle of the book, God knows why. But it's here. Something. Something Thomasina wrote."

I do not know quite why I am setting this down so many years after having abandoned my diary. I thought once, I remember, that in these pages I would record every detail of a new and extraordinary life, my life in the Forest with Atembogunjo. For some days at the beginning of our time together as wanderers in the Forest I retained, I recall now, my intention of compiling a full account of my experiences. To what end I know not. Perhaps I still nurtured the notion then that nothing has truly happened unless it has been recorded in words. Soon, however, I must have realised that I was destined for the remainder of my days, however long that might be, not to live a life in which things truly happened. I was destined to live a life wholly composed of mere happenings, each of equal value, none different from another, a flux. Certainly there was no question of writing for other eyes than my own. I was sure then, in the earliest of our days together, that my life would never again go beyond the bounds of the Forest, beyond, indeed, its innermost confines, beyond Atembogunjo's arms. Nor could I have written for him. He, of course, knows nothing of writing, or what it means. He is different from his fellow dwellers in the Forest only in that he is a wanderer, such as my tutor Manyalibo once was, though Atembogunjo left the life of his village of his own free will.

Before I had even set pencil to paper in those first days I saw, however, that anything I might write could be only an endless repetition of - of what? Of living within the Forest, of taking from it what it chose out of its glorious wildness, out of its laws iron-bound as any decree of emperor or prelate, to provide for me, for us? What could be said about that? That on Monday we ate a monkey Atembogunjo had brought down with an arrow from his bow and on Tuesday we ate the soft white grubs to be found behind the bark of a certain tree? How could one set down such things as that, living as we do in a world in which there is no Monday, no Tuesday, but only the day on which the grubs were found, the monkey came within arrow-shot? What could be said of Atembogunjo and my love for him? That one night we did this? That on one day about noon we did that? The difference in what we came to do on one day or another, I soon saw, was no more than the difference between one leaf unfolding at one time in such-and-such a manner and another unfolding on a different tree in a different manner. Neither one any more a happening to be made true by being fixed in words than the other. Each just another moment in the web of life which we are, here in the Forest, part of.

But now that I am, as Manyalibo and his fellow village dwellers used to say, dead – and likely soon, I know, to be completely dead and soon thereafter dead for ever – it has come into my mind to write something down nevertheless. So I have asked Atembogunjo to fetch for me that long-forgotten leather bag which at the start of our time together with all the possessions I had brought with me bundled into it, I had enclosed in a cairn of stones that I had begged Atembogunjo to build with me. Even then I knew in my heart that there was no purpose in preserving those things from another life. But I wished, I suppose, to keep for a little one thin line back to what I had been once, or I wished not at any one moment to cut that line. When I have finished now writing what I feel some strange, strong impulse to write – if finish it I ever shall, if I can say what, dimly, I want to say – I shall ask Atembogunjo to replace the bag in the cairn which has preserved it now for so many years. There it may stay, as safely preserved, until one day perhaps, some far, far distant day when the Forest has at last succumbed to the world of civilisation, when all the great trees have been cut down for man's use and the ground where they grew is perhaps no more than straight ploughed fields, other eyes than mine may read what I have written, what I hope now to write.

Yet what is it I have to say? This morning when I asked Atembogunjo to bring me the bag that lies at my feet now, as I sit propped against this aroko tree, I thought I knew. I had thought so for some two or three days, with increasing insistence, ever since, indeed, it had become clear to me that I was dead and soon would be dead for ever. But now that the moment has come to set down those thoughts, I baulk.

How curious it is, I reflect, that I am able to write at all, to put down words, to form letters. It has been years, many, many years, since I have written a word, since I have uttered a word of English even, almost since I have had a single thought couched in the language of my birth. Yet, no sooner was this pencil in my hand, than words, written words, those alien things, came. It must mean, I see now pausing to consider, that I am still the she who marched her way here to the heart of the Forest, who was once that young woman in Salisbury hearing in the office of the attorney in Castle Street what a large sum she had been bequeathed by her old friend Doctor Diver and who resolved there and then to go to Africa and to complete the task her mentor had never had the strength to resume himself.

How odd it is, too, that one day – it must have been five years ago, perhaps six – I did in a manner complete that task. It was by chance, purely by chance, that wandering with Atembogunjo, looking as I recall for honey, I realised I had come to the place I had striven for so long, in that other life of mine, to reach. It was as Doctor Diver had described it, exactly so. There was the yellow-fanged rock and the triple waterfall that fell from it. But the years since my old friend had found those miracle leaves there had done their work. The stream that flowed from the foot of that rock no longer meandered in such a way as to leave a small patch of swampy ground. Now it ran steadily in a deep bed it had worn for itself, and on either side the ground was dry, or as dry as it ever is under the green shade of the Forest trees. Of those plants, which I had so nearly lost my life in trying to find, there was not the slightest sign. Perhaps others of their sort grow elsewhere in the Forest. The Forest is so full of marvels and mysteries there is no telling. But I have never seen them. My quest, which seems to me now a fairy story told to me when I was a little girl tucked up in bed in that little house in the Close that was for so long home to me, that quest of mine could never have had an end.

But enough of that. I did not drag my dead body here and ask Atembogunjo to take from its hiding-place that old bag of mine just to put down on paper the ironical ending of a quest that once seemed to be so large an enterprise, a task for a lifetime. I made that effort, and it cost more than I care to think, so as to write down the thoughts that have been in my head ever since I came to realise my life was near its end.

I have a message to put into a bottle. Strange how that idea comes back to me. It must have been there in my mind ever since I was – what? – nine years old. I was nine, I remember, when mama had suffered a severe attack of the influenza and papa had sent her, together with myself, to Bournemouth to recuperate in the sea air. It was early in the summer, but the weather was fine enough for us to go down to the beach every day. There, once, mama told me about the sailors cast away upon desert islands who would place a message in a bottle and throw it into the sea. She said that sometimes such a bottle would be found and the castaway rescued. I suppose she was seeking an illustration for me of the goodness of Providence, that in all the wild wastes a call for help could be tossed to and fro until it reached a saviour. But I was interested only in the illustration, not in the lesson. Nothing would serve after that but that I, too, should put a message in a bottle and confide it to the whims of the mighty ocean.

I found a bottle – it was, I remember now clearly as if I was still in Bournemouth, a blue-glass bottle, one that had contained Thorley's tonic mixture – and I wrote my childish message out, sealed it firmly within, tossed it into the sea and, till I was quite sternly bidden back to our lodgings for tea, watched it bob and duck among the wavelets, all notions of a beneficent Providence forgotten in my delight. Later, true, I came firmly to believe that there was a Providence that guided all lives, trust in it if they would. And later still, here in Africa, I came to find that idea was somehow without meaning. Yet now, again, I am about to put a message into a bottle in the hope that one day, somehow, other eyes will see it.

So I must no longer hold back from indicting those words I have in my head.

What I have to say is what I have learned from the Forest, from the wildness of it and from the iron rules that it equally lives by. I want to declare that there is wildness and that there is order, that there are rules but that there is also 'rulelessness'. Both exist. Both have to be there. Each is right. Each is to trust. Each is wrong. Each must be distrusted. Then we have, every one of us, to find a path between this wrong and this right, this right and this wrong. For each one of us, too, that path is different. I have found mine. It is very far from the path which I thought as a girl, as a young woman, I would follow. It is far from the path which I believed I had to follow, the path laid down for a woman, in England, in the nineteenth century, the path of an ordered, conforming life.

When I first came to know the Forest I began to think the path I was to follow was the path of the wild. Nearly I did throw myself on to that path, in the days when I was tempted to stay in the village where I found Manyalibo and to cast myself, as I then thought, on the life-enhancing variety and wonderful chaos of the Forest. But it was only in my years wandering free with Atembogunjo that I have found my own path, the one, as I now believe, that each of us must find alone, setting rules to one side, rulelessness to the other. This path of mine is different from Atembogunjo's, if only by a little. To you who one day may see these words, if tossing chance brings it about, I say: there is a path for you, and it is a path that you must seek out till you have found it and tread steadily thereafter, twist and turn though it may.

EPILOGUE

Tom got up and flicked off the video.

"Is that the baby?" David asked.

"No, idiot. She's sound asleep. But you don't want to solemnly watch the credits once again, do you?"

"No. No, I suppose I can take those as read, after a couple of years. But, you know, it really wasn't a bad little film, was it? I mean, all right it never came up to first expectations. No great sexy revelations. But it had something. It caught the Forest."

"Oh, yes, it did that. Marvellous, appalling Forest. But I still wonder if it was right not to use every word Thomasina wrote in her testament."

"Oh, come on," David said. "We couldn't have done that. Not in a film that had to be sold in the nature slot. What would Mrs. Reg Blandy have made of *each is right. Each is to trust. Each is wrong. Each must be distrusted*? Little Reg would have had a hard time explaining that!"

"Yes, I know. But I still feel in a way that we owed it to Thomasina, to put those words of hers we discovered into our programme and not just leave them for that piece in the *Sunday Messenger.*"

"Because of what they did for us?"

"Yeah. I mean, they did do a lot for us. I don't suppose without them we'd have ever taken the plunge into matrimony. She gave us, to quote Conrad, your favourite: a kind of light. Poor Thomasina."

"Oh, I'm not belittling her. Not one bit. I always said she was a pretty terrific lady, and I thought so in spades after I'd read and read what she had to say about the path between order and chaos. I mean, without her we'd never have plumped for as much of order as we have. That's for sure."

"But..."

Tom wrinkled in doubt the piquant wedge-shaped face the TV millions saw now only in the quiz show *Where in the World?*

"But have we left in too much chaos in our way of life?" she said. "Have I? Have you?"

"Are you suggesting that though life après marriage is pretty splendid, there may be life après divorce to come?"

"Well, it could happen, couldn't it? I mean, it just could."

David gave a rueful smile and grasping her hand said, "Better cross fingers then. Or something."

ENDEAVOUR INK

Endeavour Ink is an imprint of Endeavour Press.

If you enjoyed *A Kind of Light* check out
Endeavour Press's eBooks here:
www.endeavourpress.com

For weekly updates on our free and discounted eBooks sign up
to our newsletter:
www.endeavourpress.com

Follow us on Twitter:
@EndeavourPress